Fallana Sian

Galessel's Tale Vol. 3
An Ashelon Novel

Books by Carolyn Kay

Dien-Vek: Galessel's Tale Volume 1

Sikevra: Galessel's Tale Volume 2

Fallana Sian: Galessel's Tale Volume 3

Meet Me on Bandon IV

Fallana Sian

Galessel's Tale Vol. 3
An Ashelon Novel

Carolyn Kay

Ashelon Publishing

Cover art, design, and interior illustrations Copyright © 2020 by Chaz Kemp.
Interior design by Carolyn Kay
Editors: Aimee Heckel, Sam Knight

ISBN 13: 978-0-9987071-7-4

1. Fantasy 2. Steampunk

First Edition: 2020

Printed in the United States of America

www.worldofashelon.com

Those with privilege and means must stand up for those who still struggle.

Acknowledgements

This book wouldn't be what it is without the help of my steadfast husband, Chaz. He built the framework of this story from which I hung the words. This is as much his baby as it is mine. He was involved from start to finish: from outlining, to chapter reviews, beta reading, and of course all of the art. He is my go-to when I get stuck and when I just can't find the right way to say something. I can't thank him enough. I also owe a debt of gratitude to my critique group: John, Jennifer, Sarah, and Robbie. Your kind and thoughtful reviews were invaluable. A huge thank you goes out as well to Aimee and Sam, my editors. I promise to work on my comma problem. And lastly, a warm thank you to my fans, family, and friends. You are amazing, and I love you all.

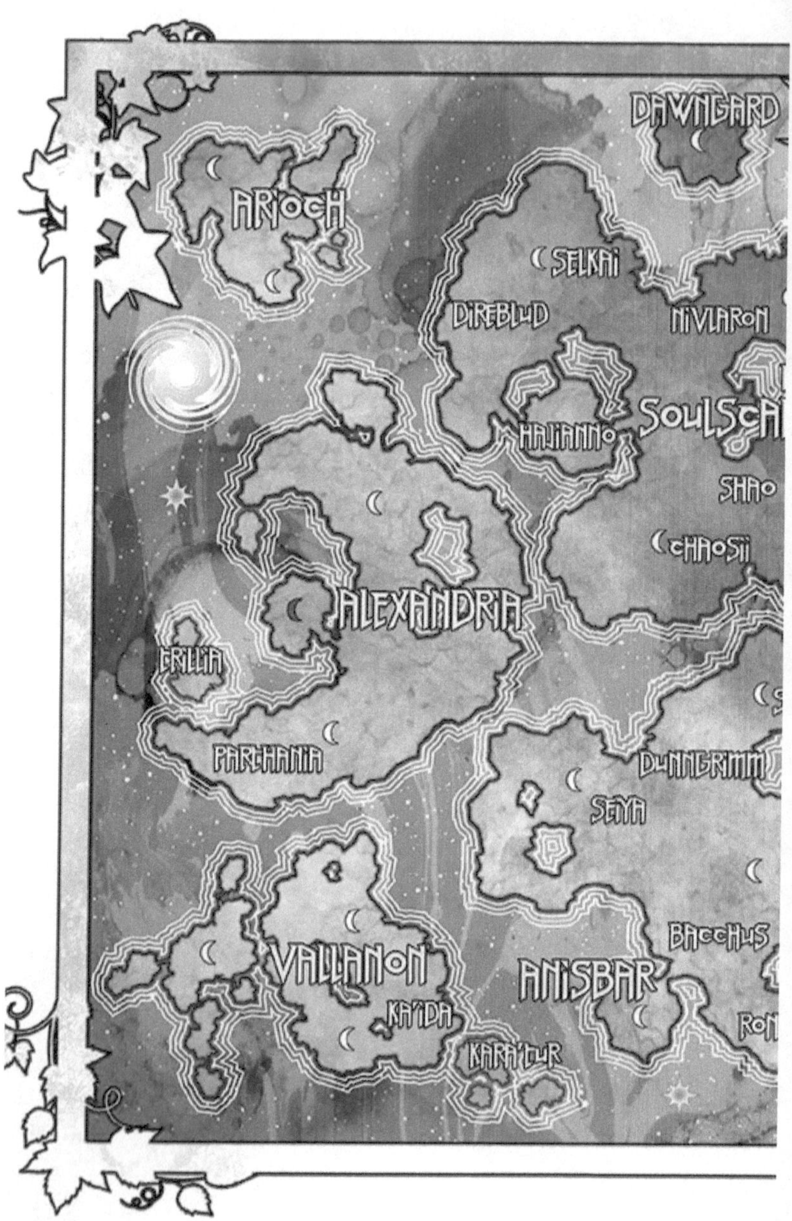

DAWNGARD
ARIOCH
SELKAI
DIREBLUD
NIVIARON
SOULSCAR
HAIIANNO
SHAO
CHAOSII
ALEXANDRIA
CRILLIA
PARCHANIA
DUNNGRIMM
SEYA
VALLANON
ANISBAR
BACCHUS
KAIDA
KARATUR
ROM

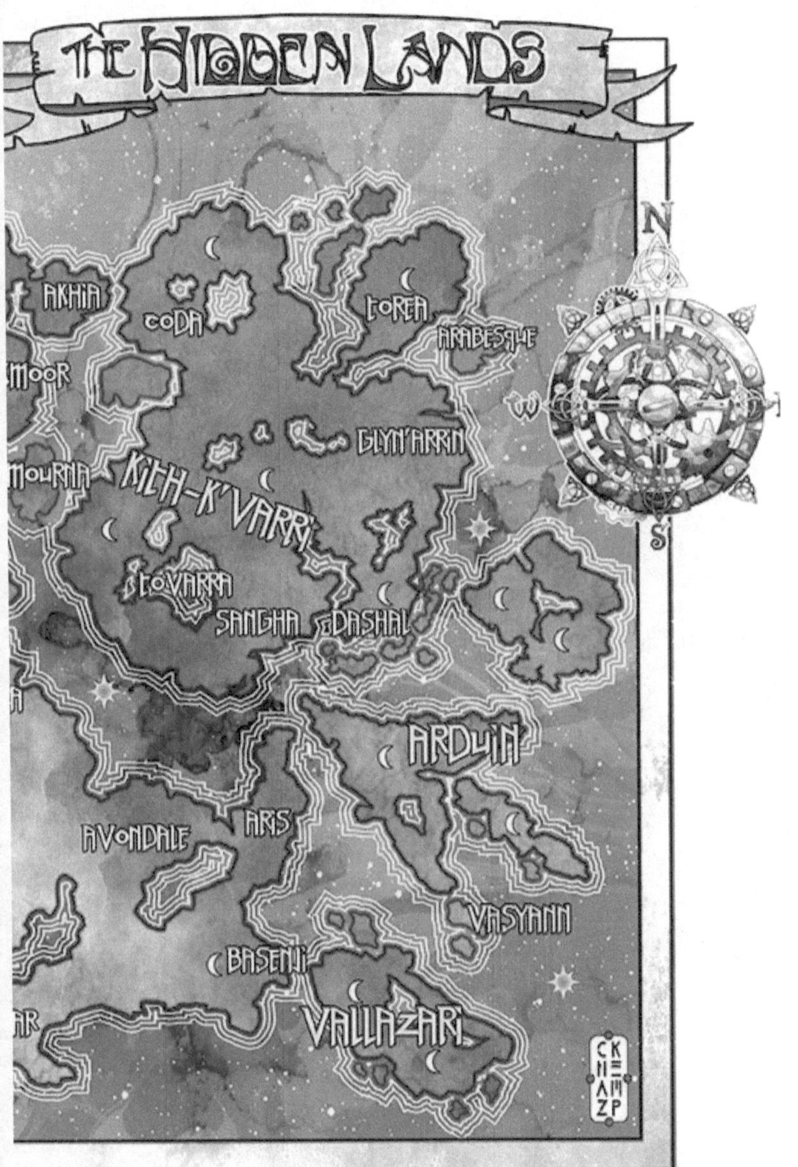
THE HIDDEN LANDS
N
S
E
W
AKHIA
CODA
LOREA
ARABESQUE
MOOR
MOURNA
KIEH-K'VARRI
GLYN'ARRAN
LOVARRA
SANGHA
DASHAL
ARDUIN
AVONDALE
ARIS
VASYANN
BASENJI
VALLAZARI

THE EMPIRE OF
ASHELON
THE YEAR 1850
FOSNA
SVERIGG
LOHJA
SKOTIA
EIRE
ASHELON
SKANE
PRUSSIA
BAVASIA
KIEVKA
GALLIA
SKITAZRA
DEVA
CATALAN
ESPERIA
HELLAS

Prologue
Arturia

Queen Victoria took a shallow breath, inhaling the vapor from the mask she was now forced to wear when not in her hyperbaric chamber. Professor Iterol had worked with Dr. Jekyll to perfect the formula which kept her illness—some new form of consumption—from killing her. She hated the way the sickly sweet vapor slid into her lungs and crawled around inside her. Victoria shook away the thought. She would endure, if only to spite those who would see her dead.

A bell rang. Victoria spun her mechanized chair to face the door of her private chamber as her valet, Aiden, opened it.

From the doorway her chamberlain announced, "Lord Davorin and Captain Kane, your majesty." The greying statesman then stepped aside.

The Svellvegan lord was first into the room, gliding in on soft-soled boots, silent and cunning as a wolf. His purple velvet coat billowed around his tall, muscular frame and his black hair was pulled back in a queue at the nape of his neck. Judging by the goggles settled above the brim of his deep purple top hat, he'd come straight from the airfield.

Davorin stopped at the barest respectful distance, removed his hat with a flourish, and bowed just barely at the waist; it was a slight, but Victoria ignored it. She'd be done with him soon enough.

"Your majesty," he said in his slick, elven accent. Without the magic of the ice diamond, the thrill his voice used to give her was gone. "Your color is better than when I beheld you last. My commendations to your doctors."

His smirk did nothing to hide the malice Victoria knew was there. Davorin's people despised weakness of any kind. If she were his queen, he likely would have killed her and taken her throne. But she wasn't, and he didn't.

He set his top hat on her desk with an air of indifference and sat in the tall-backed chair across from her.

If Davorin was akin to a wolf, Captain Kane, leader of the Hammer Guardians, was a bulldog; stout, loyal, and brutish, with a nose flattened from brawling. Kane had stomped in behind Davorin, making no attempt to emulate the elf's grace and barely remembered to remove his bowler before bowing.

"Your majesty," he said in a voice ground to gravel by too many cigars.

The scent of the vapor from her mask was preferable to the stench of cheap cigars and stale whiskey she knew emanated from Kane. He took a seat, his hands clenching his bowler, clearly uncomfortable in polite company.

Victoria took a breath of vapor, then removed the mask. Speaking through it made her sound like she was talking from the bottom of a metal well and that just wouldn't do.

Aiden took it from her, looping the tubing around a hook on the back of her wheeled chair. He set the mask in its compartment before melting back into the shadows of her private chamber.

Foregoing pleasantries to save her breath, Victoria got right to the point of this audience. "I have considered your request, Lord Davorin, and while your plan to invade the Hidden Lands intrigues me, your missive was short on details. I am curious, why is this gryphon you call Soji such a threat? I have seen the one Marquis Beauvau has mounted in his ballroom in Calais. It is not much bigger than a lion, and he claims to have killed it with a simple hydronium hunting rifle. Why do you need a contingent of my men and cold-iron weapons?"

Davorin laughed, sending icicles down Victoria's spine. She detested the Svellvega elf, but he was a necessary means to an end. After an enlightening audience with Princess Galessel, nearly a year ago, she'd rid herself of the ice diamond Davorin had given her. Something the traitorous she-elf had said about it rang true. Things she'd later learned about Davorin had reinforced the need to be rid of the thing. Since then, she'd been even more cautious around him.

"Soji is no common gryphon, m'lady," Davorin said. "It is enormous, easily ten times the size of one of your elephants, and as formidable as a dragon. It's been the protector of the Anisbarii throne for millennia and can be summoned to their aid with the snap of a finger—if you believe the legends. No one's seen the beast in generations."

"And yet," Kane growled, "you believe this creature exists and is worth risking my men, and rare cold-iron, to search it out and destroy it?" Kane growled. Victoria could always rely on Kane to be direct.

Davorin leaned forward, resting his forearms on his knees. The thick gold ring in the top of his left ear flashed in the lamp light. Ignoring Kane, he addressed Victoria. "I don't have to believe. We've found it. The beast nests in a remote floating island between the realms of Arduin and Vallazari. With your men safely hidden within a disguised airship, it should be rather easy to fly there. A few cannonballs laced with cold-iron will kill it.

"Once it's no longer a threat, your troops can infiltrate the Anisbarii palace, kill the royal family, and take the keys to the Moon Gates. With those keys, we can bring in the rest of your Hammer Guardians and our respective armies. Together we can take the Hidden Lands in a matter of days."

"And what's to keep you from killing my men and keeping the cold-iron and the Hidden Lands to yourself?" Kane asked.

Davorin turned to him, disdain for the man plain on his face. "Nothing."

He straightened in the chair and smoothed a fold in his coat. "We could easily kill your men, take the cold-iron and go on with the plan, but admittedly, we need the might of the Ashelonian army to fully take the Hidden Lands." He nodded toward Victoria. "Besides, we've agreements to uphold. The Svellvega keep their word."

Kane moved to argue, but Victoria held up her hand. Kane closed his mouth so quickly his teeth clicked.

Victoria could feel a cough building in her lungs and took shallower breaths to suppress it. Even with the agreements in place, which were heavily in the Svellvega's favor, she didn't trust Davorin not to try something. She didn't let it concern her. She had plans of her own. "Very well. I trust the two of you can finalize the details of this endeavor without me?"

They both nodded, standing at the obvious dismissal. Davorin picked up his hat, placed it on his head with a flourish, and bowed once again. "A pleasure, your majesty. I will send word when the task is complete. In the meantime, prepare your army. They may have cold-iron, but the creatures they'll face in the Hidden Lands are dangerous and cunning, and your men need to be ready."

Victoria waved him off, succumbing to the cough. The handkerchief covering her mouth came away bloody. Dr. Jekyll's vapor was keeping the disease at bay, but only just.

She didn't hear Davorin leave, but she did hear her chamber door close.

Kane cleared his throat, surprising Victoria. She though he'd left with Davorin.

"Mum, pardon my boldness," he said, "but you know the Svellvega will likely kill my men once we've taken the palace. They've no love for humans, and our reports say they've been recruiting other races into their army. Even if they do need us to conquer the Hidden Lands, what's to stop them from turning on us and invading Ashelon?"

Wracked by another cough, Victoria couldn't respond. Aiden rushed to her side and dutifully unwound the tubing and helped her place the mask back over her face. Victoria inhaled the slippery vapor and instantly felt the tremors in her lungs subside.

"And why did you not confront Davorin about the poison?" Kane asked. His voice held a hint of a growl, much like a guard dog caught between its master and a stranger it wasn't sure if it should bite.

"Why?" Her voice sounded like she was speaking through a metal can. "He and I both know what he did. Besides, the doctors say the poison has a root in magic. When we destroy the Hidden Lands and its magic, the poison should be rendered inert. If you can trust the ravings of a mad scientist."

She shrugged. "And if it does not, I will have still gotten my revenge and can die satisfied that those filthy flies have been eliminated." She took another deep breath of vapor, nearly gagging on the taste it left in the back of her throat. Only a few more months of this torture and she'd be free of it. Assuming Kane and his men did their job.

"As for your first question: I'm well aware the Svellvega will likely turn on us once they've taken the Hidden Lands. That's why I have a different mission for you and your men."

Kane took his seat again and leaned in, eager to hear what Victoria had planned. As she laid it out for him, he grinned like a schoolyard bully who'd just found his next mark.

Victoria, exhausted from speaking, waved her dismissal.

Kane rose and bowed, attempting a flourish with his hat like Davorin and almost succeeding. "Asher's blessing be upon you, mum." He grinned again. "Those flies will never know what hit them."

He headed for the door, his step noticeably lighter.

Chapter 1
Death's Embrace

Kane looked nervously at the clouds passing quickly below them. He didn't have much stomach for heights, but he couldn't back down when Davorin invited him out to the rail to see the Sun Gate. No high-nosed elf would get the better of him.

Death's Embrace was the sleekest airship he'd ever seen: all black with inlays of silver and ice-blue glass. It was too bad it was of Svellvegan make. The balloon was silver, not the typical black the Svellvega favored, and shaped like a bullet. It flew no colors, but it was obvious this wasn't a typical fly airship, or a human one for that matter. It was built for speed. Smaller and more streamlined than a typical military airship, most of the room onboard was reserved for its six cannons, four hydronium-powered Gatling guns, and all of the requisite ammunition.

Kane noted, from Davorin's loquacious ramblings during the journey to the airfield, the crew slept standing up to provide more room for munitions.

There was a decided lack of crew on deck. He'd only counted five above deck so far. There were a few well-muscled Svellvega adjusting lines fore and aft, one cranking a wheel to close up a hatch in the deck, and one at the bow, singing what sounded a bit like the drinking songs he and his mates would belt out at the pub, but that was it.

He'd met the captain on the enclosed bridge when he'd first boarded. The elf was alone in a room full of buttons, levers, and other mechanical contraptions that looked like they'd be better suited for a factory than the bridge of an airship.

"You might want to hold on to the rail, Kane," Davorin drawled in his pretentious accent. "The portal's just ahead, and I'm told humans tend to be nauseated by the transit."

Kane shrugged. "I'm not some milk-fed girl, Davorin. I've sailed on ships in the worst of the maelstroms that come up from Freedonia. Some magic portal isn't going to turn me green."

"Suit yourself." Davorin shrugged, pulling his goggles down from his top hat.

"Pointy-eared bastard," Kane thought. He knew the elf was a means to an end, but he couldn't wait to be done with him. Pulling the collar of his coat up to keep the rain off his neck, he donned his own goggles. The colored lenses turned the grey sky into an inky green, and a shimmering portal appeared ahead, where nothing had been before.

No wonder getting into the Hidden Lands was such a trick. The portals were hidden unless you had the right lenses. He'd make sure to tell the Queen about it as soon as he returned to Arturia.

Kane stared at the portal, studying it. A sickly puce, watery center was surrounded by what looked like giant, dull grey butterfly wings. A strange, vine-like tail hung down from the bottom of the thing, making the whole portal look like some kind of headless insect, and the ship was aimed directly at its liquid heart.

Fear clenched Kane's stomach into a knot as the portal loomed closer. He began to doubt his decision to come on this mission. What if going through the portal was deadly for humans? Davorin would then be in complete control of the cold-iron.

The ship lurched as the bow sliced into the liquid center of the portal. Quicker than a blink, the portal's maw engulfed the ship.

He stumbled. His bones turned to jelly then solidified again as they arrived on the other side. Kane wondered if he'd actually been run through a magical meat grinder. Everything hurt. He grabbed the rail, leaned over, and promptly lost his lunch. Wiping his mouth on the back of his sleeve, Kane caught Davorin's smirk.

He glared back but said nothing. It was the magic that got to him. All the more reason to be rid of it.

The air on this side of the portal was clear and fresh with no hint of soot, but felt somewhat thin. Weather apparently did not span between the two places.

Kane removed his goggles and gawked at the sky. He'd never seen a sky so blue, not even on the open ocean away from the smog of Arturia. It was as if the deep blue waters of the Baltic Sea were suddenly above him. Fluffy purple, pink, and white clouds drifted past as if on a slow river.

On this side, the portal was visible without the colored lenses. No longer dull and grey, it had come to life. Rainbow-hued wings pulsed slowly, and the tail swished lazily like a cat's.

As the ship pulled away, Kane rolled his shoulders back and stretched his neck to rid himself of the residual soreness left over from the portal. He didn't like the idea he might have just passed through the guts of some creature. Out of curiosity, he looked over the side of the airship but could see nothing but more of the candy floss clouds below him.

"You won't see land for another hour or so, I'm afraid," Davorin said, right in Kane's ear.

Kane flinched at Davorin's nearness—the elf had no sense of personal space—and gave him yet another glare, which seemed to roll right off the damned elf.

"Sun gates are at such a high altitude," Davorin continued, "you cannot see the surface. Come, let me show you below decks. We're going to ascend even higher so as to avoid detection, and the air will become unbreathable on the open deck without the proper equipment."

Kane followed Davorin through the door, noting the few Svellvega he'd seen before were no longer on deck.

The efficiency of design continued below deck. Lanterns, fueled by some substance unknown to Kane, filled the hold with a golden light. He smelled oiled wood and the sharp tang of iron but no hint of gas or burning oil. His thoughts were interrupted by Davorin.

"As you can see, crew quarters have been eliminated. The men sleep standing up in those cocoons over there." Davorin pointed to a series of thick, white sleeping bags standing upright, each held up against the hull by its own net. There were only six of them.

The elf grinned at Kane. "Yes, you are counting right. There are only six. This ship is so advanced and much more streamlined than any of human or Anisbarii make that it only takes ten men to run it."

Kane wanted to punch the smug look off of Davorin's face. His time would come.

He knew the crew of *Death's Embrace* was small, but could it really be manned by less than a dozen men? If so, his task just became much, much easier.

He followed Davorin farther into the hold, past crates of cold-iron swords and daggers, racks of specialized pistols made to fire cold-iron-infused steam balls, and casks of grenades that would send cold-iron shrapnel into everything within a twenty-foot radius.

Davorin prattled on about something to do with the pipes and various cables and such running along the hull and the ceiling above them. He finally paused and turned slowly around, finally seeing the casks of ammunition and grenades—and the hostile faces of the twenty-five human Hammer Guardians crowded into the hold.

"I see that, once again, Victoria has given in to her paranoia of the fae. I've seen the effectiveness of your cold-iron weapons. You will only need a small fraction of this to kill the gryphon and any fae around it."

Kane rolled his eyes. Her Highness had said Davorin was arrogant to a fault. "Well, yes, but why stop with one giant gryphon? Soji isn't the only *thing* our blessed Queen has sent us to wipe out."

Davorin's eyes widened as Kane slipped the cold-iron dagger between his ribs. The elf fell to his knees, convulsing, his skin turning a rotten green. Kane felt a mix of elation and nausea watching the overbearing elf lord, screaming, melt like a cheap candle.

"Go to hell, you *fly*. May you rot in a pool of boiling pus for poisoning our Queen."

As one, the humans nearest the elf spat in the direction of the puddle of goo and fancy clothes that used to be the Svellvegan lord. Kane swallowed back a bit of bile and focused his gaze on his men.

"Arm yourselves quickly. I don't trust that filthy fly to tell us the real number of crew. Be on your guard and shoot anything with a ring in its ear."

His men, dressed in identical black suits with buttoned waistcoats and white club collar shirts with black ties, quickly moved to do his bidding, saying little as they armed themselves from the cache in the hold.

The Hammer Guardians made quick work of the few Svellvega crew members they found. One shot, occasionally two, was all it took to incapacitate them. Kane's men relieved the elves of their breathing masks before firing a few more shots to insure the wretches melted into piles of steaming green goo.

Leaving the captain for last, Kane was a bit surprised the elf hadn't come out of the bridge to defend his men and ship. He kicked open the door, pistol leveled at the back of the captain, who, unflinchingly, kept his hands on the wheel. On either side of him, Kane heard the familiar click of three other pistols locking into firing position.

"Kane, welcome aboard," the captain said calmly. "As per our agreement, I promised to take you to Soji, and I will uphold my part of the bargain, in good time. But before you even think about double-crossing and killing me, know that I am the only one left who knows how to pilot this ship."

The arrogant bastard never turned around, but continued to fly, flipping a switch here or there before adjusting the wheel.

"Still not sure why we need you, Murik." Kane pulled back the hammer of his pistol and locked it into place. "Davorin said you only need ten men to fly this ship. I have twenty-five."

Murik turned around, holding up a hand slick with blood. Crimson dripped from the ship's wheel, forming a small puddle at Murik's feet. "Yes, but now the ship is blood-bonded to me. The controls won't work for anyone else, and really, the other men were just for security—worthless as they were. I can fly this ship single-handedly."

"Clever elf, but do you really think we'd fall for that bit of rubbish?" Any fly that would betray his own people wasn't to be trusted. Kane kept his pistol aimed at Murik.

"Of course not. You're obviously one of Victoria's best men. But let me point out I am also the only one on this ship who speaks, reads, and writes more than a dozen languages native to the Hidden Lands, and I'm the only one who knows where you need to go to do the most damage to this vile place. Killing Soji will be vital, but there is so much more you can do. I can guide you." Murik gestured around the bridge. "You may have also noticed there are no maps here or anywhere on this ship."

That certainly could be a problem. "So where are you hiding them?" He knew some captains could navigate without maps, but no captain worth his salt would leave port without at least a star chart.

"I'm not hiding them, you short-lived cretin. I threw them overboard half an hour ago. They're likely in the belly of some beast by now."

Kane had hoped to be completely free of the Svellvega once they got through the portal. He lowered his pistol and waved forward one of his men, who pulled Murik's hands behind his back. The elf stayed compliant, a sly grin on his face.

Another Hammer Guardian, a smallish man named Finnley, went to the ship's wheel. Pulling out a handkerchief, he wiped the blood off the wheel, then attempted to turn it. It wouldn't budge. He tried flipping a couple of switches. Again, nothing moved.

With a heavy sigh, Kane signaled the man holding Murik to let him go. "You're crafty, I'll give you that. I don't trust any man who'd betray his own, but I do respect your desire for destruction. So what's your plan?

Murik smiled and shook out his hands. Blood spattered across several surfaces, including Finnley's face. The small man glared daggers at Murik but said nothing. He wiped away the blood with his handkerchief, which he then dropped on the floor, disgusted.

"I need to make a stop to verify some information and test a theory," Murik said. "If I'm right, we'll be able to sow destruction all across the Hidden Lands. If I'm wrong, we'll go straight for Soji."

Kane's mistrust of Murik warred with his desire to wreak havoc on the fae. However, if a chance existed to destroy more of the enemy before the army arrived, a delay would be worth it. "Very well," Kane said. "We'll test your theory. But cross me, and I guarantee you'll end up as a puddle like the rest of your kind."

Murik waved a dismissal. "The galley's on the lowest deck," he said. "Stay away from the troll blood pudding, and settle in. We're a day out from our first stop."

CHAPTER 2
ANISBAR

Galessel wiped the sweat off her brow, thankful for the short respite from sword training. She'd come a long way in a year. When she'd started sword lessons with Navarre, shortly after he'd fled to the Hidden Lands to escape a death warrant, she'd barely been able to hold up her practice rapier for fifteen minutes. Now, after spending nearly every day training, she could spar with him for close to an hour before needing to rest. In that time, Navarre had also taught her hand-to-hand fighting, and they'd both learned to shoot nearly every hydronium gun in the armory.

It kept them from going crazy, confined as they were behind the palace walls. Galessel was still *sikevra*, branded an outcast due to her mutilated ears. The pirate responsible was still out there. Navarre chose to stay with her instead of venturing out with Clove and the small band of human rebels. He hadn't hid that his reasoning behind staying was as much personal as it was professional.

Increasing hostilities with the Svellvega had kept Galessel's parents, the king and queen of Anisbar and the Hidden Lands, from convening the *Fallana Sian*, the forgiveness ritual ceremony that would reverse her outcast status. Though they'd made a proclamation she was not, in fact, *sikevra*, not everyone in the realm would believe it. Many fae in the Hidden Lands would kill her as soon as they saw her mutilated ears. The magic of the *Fallana Sian* would tell the world the gods and assembled royalty had forgiven her. Without it, she was a criminal with only two choices: permanent exile or death.

Confined within the palace for the last year, Galessel felt like a prisoner. It gave her new appreciation for the freedoms she once enjoyed as an ambassador, and she longed for those days past.

The royal gymnasium now felt as much like home as her own room did. Unlike other rooms in the palace, the stone walls here were unadorned, keeping the room cool, which Galessel appreciated. Racks of practice weapons lined the walls: wooden swords and daggers, spears, light shields, and bows. A narrow strip along the longest wall was cordoned off as an archery range, and weights and mats were stacked in another corner for conditioning and calisthenics.

A page ran into the gymnasium. His long tunic and loose pants were dyed the sapphire blue of Galessel's House. He stopped a respectful arm's length from Galessel and bowed from the shoulders. With a measured breath he said, "Your highness, Mistress Clove has returned. You are summoned to the king's study." He straightened and gave a slight bow of his head to Navarre. "As is Master Vonai."

"*Merci*, Raibyr," Navarre replied. Grabbing towels from a nearby table, he held one out for Galessel. "Do we have time to refresh ourselves?"

"Apologies, but the king urges you to come with haste."

Galessel wiped her face and hands with the towel. Glancing down at her tunic as she set the towel aside, she noted sweat darkened the green linen in spots, but there was nothing to be done about it. If her father urged haste, the news from Clove must be dire. "Run ahead and tell them we're on our way." Raibyr nodded and left on silent feet.

"Is it too much to hope that Clove brings good news?" she joked to Navarre.

Navarre wiped the sweat from his dark skin and offered her a flagon of water. She drank deeply as he replied. "One may hope, but Chaun, the god of luck, has not been on our side of late. Come, we should go. You elves are quick, and we do not want to be far behind Raibyr."

Even with the possibility of bad news weighing down Galessel's thoughts, she couldn't help but tease Navarre. "Shall we run after him then?" She took off at a lope, knowing Navarre could easily keep up, though he'd be breathing heavily by the time they got to her father's study on the other side of the palace.

By the time Galessel and Navarre reached the king's study, it was already filled with her father's military advisers, her mother, Clove, Samga, and Morgan. Someone had brought in extra chairs from the nearby library. The normally spacious and quiet room vibrated with a din of conversation.

Morgan was the first to spot them entering the room. She and Navarre embraced, speaking rapidly to each other in Gallian. Morgan's black leather pants and fitted jacket were dusty, and her curly locks were disheveled. Galessel looked for Clove, and spotted her friend behind several others, deeper in the study. She went to her, touching her lightly on the shoulder to get her attention.

Clove turned and gave her a hug. "Galey! Took you long enough. Raibyr said he found you and Navarre getting sweaty," she teased.

Galessel didn't have a chance to respond. Her father whistled, two short, high-pitched tones; a signal he used often with his troops to get their attention. It jarred Galessel to hear it indoors, reminding her they were at war.

The room immediately fell silent.

"Please take your seats everyone," her father, King Valandil, said. His tone was clipped, something Galessel noticed he did when he spent too long in the field with the soldiers.

Everyone found a chair. Galessel sat next to Samga, giving her a nod of greeting. The archer from Shenzhou looked as road-weary as Morgan. Mud coated the hem of her quilted pants, and her coat sleeves were torn. Unlike

Morgan, Samga's black braid was perfectly plaited. Galessel wasn't sure how she managed it. There was never a hair out of place.

Clove joined Valandil at his desk in front of the half-circle of attendees. Clove, too, was dusty, making her unusually drab garb even more so. The news must be truly bad for them to have made such obvious haste to deliver it.

"As there is no need for introductions," Valandil began. "I will only tell you that Clove and her compatriots were tasked with discovering the ways in which the Svellvega were recruiting within the Hidden Lands. Unfortunately, they discovered much more than that. Clove, if you would." Valandil stepped aside and perched on the edge of his carved bluestone desk.

Galessel wasn't sure if it was the dim lighting in the study or not, but her father looked pale.

"Your majesties," Clove began, looking at Galessel, her mother, and her father in turn. "And good folk. I wish I had better news to report." Her faun ears drooped behind the curls of her horns. "The Svellvega have now convinced the goblins of the Deep Rift to join them, and they're currently waging small-scale attacks against the mountain trolls. The trolls consider them a nuisance at the moment, but the goblin numbers are unknown so it may only be a matter of time before they become a problem. Gomar, the leader of the High Mountain clan, did tell us his scouts saw a black airship, with the Svellvega ice bear emblazoned upon its sails, descend into the Rift about a month before the goblins began attacking."

At the mention of the black airship, Galessel felt the world tilt. A ship of that same description was responsible for the attack on *The Intrepid*, more than a year ago—the attack that left her disfigured.

A high-pitched whine filled her ears, blocking out what Clove was saying. Galessel closed her eyes and breathed deeply, attempting to quell the panic attack.

Galessel felt pressure on her wrist, and the whine disappeared, but the room was quiet. The attacks had lessened, due in part, she thought, to the martial training she was doing with Navarre, but news of Svellvega ships in the Hidden Lands still made her pulse quicken and her ears ache.

Clove was no longer speaking and was looking at her with concern. Galessel looked to her wrist to find Samga pressing two fingers into the center of it. Samga smiled and released her grip.

"Better?" she asked.

Galessel took another deep breath and nodded.

"Good. Next time, you can do this yourself." Samga took Galessel's hand in hers, placing two fingers in the center of the opposite wrist. "Press here, and breathe deeply, as you did before. The ghosts will pass quickly."

Galessel did feel better and less unfocused than she normally would be after an attack. She looked around the room and felt her cheeks flush. Everyone was looking at her. It wasn't the first time, but it was embarrassing nonetheless.

"Forgive me, my friend," she said to Clove." I'm afraid I may have missed something after you said the trolls saw a black airship?"

Clove nodded. "The trolls weren't the only ones to see a black ship in recent months. Others, north of the troll's mountains, have reported seeing it, and the selkies on Arabesque Island said they saw it off the coast, but it turned away before it reached land." Clove paused, visibly collecting herself before continuing. "The fire drakes reported that not only are the Svellvega actively recruiting the nightsteeds, but they tried to recruit the drakes, as well."

Galessel shuddered. "Can I ask the obvious question? What are the Svellvega up to? Even with all the beings they've recruited, they are still outnumbered, should they march as an organized army."

"According to the drakes, they're also counting on human troops from Ashelon, and they want to wipe out the Anisbarii."

A collective gasp went up from those assembled. Queen Victoria's designs to invade the Hidden Lands and plunder it for resources had been foiled a year ago by Galessel, Clove, Navarre, and his compatriots. They'd found the massive warehouse where Victoria had stockpiled aid and supplies sent by the Hidden Lands—supplies meant for the fae and poor of Ashelon. Once discovered, Navarre's underground network distributed the goods to those in need, thus denying them to the Ashelonian army.

Clove nodded to Galessel's father, who stood and faced the assembly. "We know from Galessel's time in Ashelon that the Svellvega were working with Victoria. We thought the Ashelonian invasion plan had been halted, but obviously we were wrong. If the Svellvega manage to bring in Victoria's armies, it would give them a sizeable advantage."

"How sizeable?" Ilvisar Nerinan, her father's top general, asked. Even sitting, he towered over those next to him. A scar along his right cheek pulled his mouth into a perpetual smirk. His dark hair had been streaked with silver for as long as Galessel had known him, and instead of softening his appearance, it added an additional edge of steel to the imposing elf.

"Navarre, you know the state of Victoria's armies better than any of us here. I'm afraid Miniel's last report as ambassador was more than a year ago." Valandil motioned for Navarre to come forward.

"Your majesty." Navarre bowed to the king of the Anisbarii before facing the others. "My knowledge of her actual numbers is not much more recent than your daughter's, but I do know how she deploys them. Queen Victoria has more than one hundred fifty thousand troops, but they are spread around the mortal world to fortify Ashelon's numerous colonies. Realistically, based on the supplies we discovered last year, I would say she can spare no more than fifty thousand—if they were able to restock their supplies. If they could not, then a host of thirty thousand might be as much as she can reasonably supply."

"Then let us pray she could not resupply her armies," Ilvisar commented, his dark face unreadable. "However, I see a flaw in the Svellvega logic. What do they have on the humans that would prevent them from betraying those bastard elves as soon as they set foot in the Hidden Lands?"

"Nothing," Navarre replied. "As I see it, both armies will seek to use the other until the Hidden Lands fall, then it will simply be a matter of who has the better numbers. However, knowing how ruthless the Svellvega are, they will put the humans at the front of the army, using them as shields in the first waves of attack, and in the process, greatly reduce the Ashelonian numbers and gain the upper hand in the aftermath."

"If the Svellvega are as ruthless as you say," Samga added, "and they employ archers or any type of artillery, it's likely they'll target enemy troops and human alike."

Many in the room nodded their agreement.

Galessel overheard Morgan whisper to Samga, "You're ruthless, but I like the way you think."

Samga smiled, then addressed the group. "Eire, Skotia, and Gallia have large fae communities. Can we send word to them of Victoria's plans? If they begin to build up troops along the Ashelonian borders, it would force Victoria to hold more troops back."

Galessel tried to stay focused as the discussion of troop numbers and tactics went on, but her mind felt a little fuzzy—likely the result of her panic attack. It was hard to block the vision of the black airship from her mind, so she continued to press her fingers into her wrist. It helped some, as did trying to follow the discussion. Navarre had tried to teach her battlefield tactics, but she was much better with one-on-one negotiations than big-picture battles. As the discussion transitioned into whether the Seelie and Unseelie kingdoms would aid Anisbar, Galessel's stomach dropped a little, and she felt the need to speak up.

"The Unseelie will not come to our aid," she interrupted. "Not while there's a price on my head for insulting Prince Rhazien."

"Queen Lorelei and I have some history," Queen Annalinde responded as she stood and moved to stand by her husband. "I may be able to convince her that siding with us is advantageous to her realm."

"That may be difficult, your majesty," Clove said, her ears drooping even farther. "We also heard rumors the Unseelie may side with the Svellvega and perhaps have already been working with them for quite a while."

"Be that as it may, it is worth at least sending a missive to Lorelei. The Svellvega would see her bend a knee to them if they succeed, and that is not something Lorelei would do without a fight. She is not likely to send her subjects into one war, only to have to fight another right after."

"Your majesties, aren't we forgetting one very critical key?" Ilvisar asked. He was pacing at the back of the room, one arm crossed while the other hand cradled his chin. "Should the Svellvega attack, with or without the Ashelonian army, Soji will come to our aid, and the invasion literally turns to dust."

Galessel, confused, looked to her parents as they considered Ilvisar's statement. Soji was a myth—a story told to children to keep them in their beds at night. Her sisters had told her stories of the giant gryphon who supposedly protected the royal family, but on rare occasions was also known to eat a naughty princess or two. She didn't understand why Ilvisar was taking a children's tale so seriously.

"You know as I do, Ilvisar, that Soji will not fight our wars for us. They will protect the palace, and the royal family, should we join the battle, but they will not engage our enemies otherwise," Valandil said.

What her father said swam around in Galessel's mind like a trapped selkie. Soji was real. She chided herself for not taking the stories seriously, especially the one her mother used to tell her. But then again, having never seen the gryphon, why would she? She returned her attention to the conversation as Ilvisar continued to pace.

"Aye, but you are the high king and queen of the Hidden Lands. To rule over the entirety of the realm, the royal family must be eliminated. If any of you survive, the loyal races will not concede. Therefore, the Svellvega must take the palace, which means Soji will engage. Should the gryphon choose to, they could easily wipe out the armies with their magic, or at the very least, age them to the point of being ineffectual."

"Do the Svellvega know about this gryphon and its magic? Am I understanding that it can age creatures into death?" Navarre asked. His brow was furrowed, and Galessel thought he looked as confused as she'd felt just moments earlier.

"Yes, though to most without long life, Soji is a legend, and knowledge of their powers is either greatly exaggerated or forgotten. But the Svellvega would remember them well enough," Annalinde said. "And yes, if Soji breathes their magic on anything, it will age.

How much it ages is up to Soji."

Morgan raised her hand, waiting to catch Ilvisar's eye before asking, "You use the terms 'they' and 'them' when referring to Soji. Those aren't words we use in Ashelon when we talk about a single person. Is Soji male or female, or something else?"

"Soji is both male *and* female, but it is a long story, better told before a warm fire," Valandil responded. Navarre and the other humans did not look any less perplexed after the explanation.

Galessel furrowed her brow and bit her lip. She had so many questions about the gryphon but stayed quiet. She didn't want the assembled company to know she'd never suspected Soji was real. She planned on cornering her parents later. Another thought popped into her head. It wiggled around and slipped through her mind like a worm, evading capture. By the time she caught it, Navarre was speaking again.

"Then we must assume that Soji will be a target of the Svellvega. Possibly sooner rather than later," Navarre surmised.

A murmur spread through the room as people considered Navarre's statement. Galessel stood to get everyone's attention. "What if the humans bring cold-iron into the Hidden Lands? We destroyed what weapons they had in the cache, but what if they made more? Wouldn't Soji be a prime target?"

"The Svellvega would never agree to bring cold-iron into the Hidden Lands. It's as dangerous to them as the rest of us," Ilvisar said.

Navarre shook his head. "What if they didn't know? I would not underestimate the depths to which Victoria's armies would sink. If they still have cold-iron, they will not hesitate to use it."

"Then we must get word of the danger to Soji." Valandil rose to his feet, and the rest of the room stood in response. "Ilvisar, gather several of your best men. I will prepare a missive for them to deliver. The rest of you prepare for a Svellvega attack farther into our lands than before. Make sure your garrisons are alert and supplied. That is all."

Everyone left the room, conversing and trading battle plans. Galessel nodded for Navarre and Clove to go on without her and waited until the room was empty before confronting her father. "When were you going to tell me that Soji was real? And if you can summon them to aid us, why not do that instead of sending soldiers with a message?"

"Enough, daughter." Her father laughed. "We assumed your sisters would have told you long ago, but apparently they thought it more fun to keep you in the dark. My apologies.

"The truth of Soji is a well-guarded secret because they are such a formidable weapon. While they are capable of defending themselves with ease, the constant barrage of enemies seeking to weaken the Anisbarii throne would have eventually driven them away, or worse yet, caused them to eliminate a large portion of the Hidden Lands' populace. It is better that they remained a legend." He took Galessel's hand, leading her to a set of chairs, and sat down. "As for summoning Soji, the truth is, we cannot. Not at the moment anyway."

He shook out his wrist, and a delicate silver chain, with a small gryphon charm, slipped down to his hand. It was something Galessel had seen so often, she'd forgotten about it. Her mother had an identical one. She'd always assumed it was some sort of love token between the two of them. "This charm, and the one your mother wears, can only be activated when we are in grave, mortal danger. It will not call Soji otherwise, thus the need to send an envoy."

Galessel knew it was a long shot, but she asked anyway. "I'd like to go on the mission to warn Soji."

Her father held her hand and looked at her for a long moment. His eyes strayed to her mutilated ears, and his face filled with sadness. "My daughter, my courageous and stubborn daughter. It hurts me to keep you here, confined to the palace. Even as a child you pushed against the confines of palace life. I know you ache to leave, to do something to aid your people, and normally, you would be the first I'd think of to lead this mission, but I'm afraid I must deny your request. Even Soji would see you as *sikevra* and would likely kill you. I cannot take that risk. I'm sorry."

Galessel wanted to argue but knew it would be pointless. Though her father's eyes were liquid with unshed tears, his expression held an edge she knew meant he would brook no arguments. Not even her silver tongue would work to change his mind. Sighing, she stood, kissed him on the cheek, and left the room.

Chapter 3
Anisbar

"**N**avarre watched Galessel pace around the small, walled garden enclosure. Clove sat across from him at the small table, her large faun ears relaxed against her horns.

"Ugh! I'm so tired of being stuck in the palace," Galessel complained. Her black braid whipped around every time she spun on her heel. Now that Samga was back, Navarre thought he would have to see if the archer would teach Galessel how to weaponize her hair. It could come in handy in close-quarters combat.

Whether a trick of the muted light in the garden, or just coincidence, the white streak in Galessel's hair amplified the redness in her face. She reminded Navarre of a she-devil painting by Voltaire he'd seen in the palace at Versailles. Navarre hadn't seen Galessel so up in arms in nearly a year. Then again, she had just found out Clove and others were being sent out to determine the scope of the Svellvega's incursion, and that she still would not be allowed to join them.

Navarre understood her anger and desire to do something. He felt the same. Staying behind to train Galessel had not been a wasted effort—far from it—but it was time to test her in the real world, and he was anxious to rejoin his cohorts as well.

"Galey, I *know* you're dying to do something, I do," Clove said. The faun drew a rune on the side of a cup of coffee with her finger. A lovely scent of lavender and honey filled the little garden space as the coffee began steaming. She wrapped her hands around the cup and held it close.

The little bits of daily magic here never ceased to fascinate Navarre.

"But you know things are still dangerous out there," Clove continued. "Rhazien has increased the bounty on your head, and there are new rumors of a violent *sikevra* terrorizing small communities across the islands. A rumor Rhazien started no doubt, and the Svellvega are spreading, claiming the Anisbarii won't do anything about it, but they will."

Galessel's face got even redder at the news. "What? How? Ugh!" She threw her hands in the air. "But folk know I'm not a true *sikevra*. How many communities have I met with, have I helped with some matter or another over the years? How can they think I've turned evil?"

Navarre stood and slowly approached Galessel. He knew she could react like a cornered rabbit if surprised. Wrapping his arms around her, he kissed the top of her head. "*Mon amour*, rumors are a vile thing, spreading like disease when given a chance to take hold. Much is happening across the Hidden Lands, and the isolated nature of so many of the races here means that whatever they hear first is more likely to be taken as truth if there's nothing to refute it."

He released Galessel but kept a hand on her back and guided her to a chair around the carved table. The carvings in the table were so expertly done—interwoven knot work and fantastical animals covered the piece— he wondered if it had actually been grown that way. He wouldn't have been surprised if it was. Galessel sat but stayed on the edge of her seat.

"Clove," he said. "I do not doubt the dangers outside the palace have multiplied since I first arrived here, but so too have Galessel's fighting skills. She is more than capable of defending herself and others.

The faun smirked, looking from Galessel to Navarre. "Oh, I'm sure she's improved at a lot of things since I've been gone." She laughed, the sound something like a soft snort and a giggle.

Navarre smiled, but Galessel glared at Clove, clearly not in a mood to be jested with.

"If you doubt her abilities, Clove, then why not test her?"

Clove shrugged and set down her coffee. "Sure. Why not? We could both stand to blow off some excess energy." She rang a small bell. A female elf in palace livery seemed to flow out of a shadow near a golden oak tree. "Maela, will you get two practice swords from the gymnasium please?" The elf nodded and melted back into the shadows.

That particular trick of the palace staff still gave Navarre the chills.

Placing her hand over Galessel's, Clove said, "Galey, you know I would give anything to get you out of here, but it's not up to me." The faun's ears fell just a little, and her nose twitched.

Some of the rage left Galessel's lithe form. Her shoulders relaxed, and her color started to return to normal. "I know, my friend. It's just so frustrating. No one, especially my father, seems to have any faith in me anymore."

"I'm not sure it's a lack of faith. More that they don't want to chance losing you. They almost lost you twice. Why tempt Chaun a third time?"

"Because this time we wouldn't be tempting Chaun. I can hold my own now." Galessel stood and took the wooden swords from the elf who'd appeared behind her. She tossed one to Clove and moved through a break in the walled enclosure into a more open garden area.

Clove shrugged and raised an eyebrow to Navarre, looking for advice.

He smiled. "Test her. She's been sparring with me and her guards; I would like to see how she engages an opponent with a different skill set." The faun smiled and bounded after Galessel. Navarre followed, curious to see how his pupil would fare against someone with greater speed and a different physique.

Navarre leaned against a smooth-barked silver tree watching as Galessel and Clove faced each other across an open green space edged by low bushes in bloom with azure flowers scented of honey and citrus.

Galessel took up a fencer's stance: her right foot forward, left foot behind and at a right angle. She held her left hand up and back, behind her, while keeping the sword in her right, pointed low. Her stance was light. She looked ready to spring forward at any moment. Clove, on the other hand, stood mostly upright. As a faun, she was always on her toes—hooves—but she, too, looked ready to spring. Sword held at a higher angle, her off hand was held behind her back.

Were they on the street, Navarre would bet Clove had a dagger hidden at the small of her back, tucked into a hidden sheath within her wide leather belt. She could grab it in an instant to block a strike or throw at her opponent. Navarre hoped she did have a knife. He'd like to see how Galessel would react.

Clove feinted with a lunge, and Galessel reacted, bringing her sword up to meet Clove's, but she wasn't drawn off balance. The two sparred, wooden swords knocking with each hit. They seemed evenly matched until Clove managed to get in close. She used her sword to block an overhand strike by Galessel and with lightning quickness, pulled a dagger from her belt, striking with it—stopping short, of course—but drawing Galessel's attention to the blade at her belly.

Navarre clapped, unable to hold in a chuckle, earning a glare from Galessel.

"Damn." Galessel swore. "I should have known you'd have a dagger, *and* that you'd use it."

Clove laughed. "You've got them, too, you know."

Galessel nodded, but didn't reach for the dagger Navarre knew was tucked into her boot.

"Again." Galessel took up a ready position a little closer to Clove than before.

This time the round lasted a bit longer. Until Clove pulled her in again, this time feinting a headbutt to end it.

Galessel straightened her sleeves and looked to Navarre. "All this time, and we didn't think of headbutts as a possible countermove?"

Navarre cocked an eyebrow at her. "We? I might not have ever used it against you, but that is not to say I did not think about it. I expected it would be the first thing you think about when your opponent has horns like a ram."

Clove hopped about a bit and mocked primping her horns. "These aren't just for attracting satyrs you know."

Galessel smiled and went back to her ready stance. "Again."

Navarre watched with admiration as Galessel and Clove danced in the garden, trading move and countermove, neither letting the other get close this time. Incrementally, they began to move faster and faster.

"I think you've been holding out on me, Galey," Clove noted after one particularly intense exchange.

"So have you, my friend," Galessel replied.

They continued to spar, trading blows at an even faster pace. This time, Navarre noticed Galessel using a series of moves intended to deliberately pull Clove in closer. As they clinched swords, Galessel said, "Wow, you're really slow, Clove."

Clove's eyes flashed silver, and she began to move as if she was stuck in molasses. Galessel easily disarmed her and held her sword to her friend's throat. "Concede?"

Clove nodded, ducking back from Galessel's sword. "No fair, Galey. You used your silver tongue on me."

"All's fair in love and war, Clove," Navarre said.

"Well done, the both of you. But it appears Navarre

still has more to teach you, Galessel. I think you need to get a little dirtier," Morgan said, startling everyone.

Even Navarre had been so engrossed in the sparring match that he'd missed his friend's entrance into the garden. Of course, Morgan was more than skilled when it came to sneaking, but Navarre wasn't sure she'd been trying this time. He chided himself for not noticing her. Too long with in the safety of the palace, he'd let his guard down.

Clove snorted at Morgan's remarks. To cover her mirth, she took a towel from a liveried elf, and made a show of wiping off her face. She sobered quickly though, saying, "Nice trick with the silver tongue, but you know that won't work on everyone—especially the Svellvega."

Smiling, Galessel toweled her face and neck. "My grandmother showed me a few tricks that will work regardless of my opponent's race." Her smile faded. "But none of that matters if I'm stuck here in the palace."

Clove cocked an ear and chewed her lower lip for a moment. "What if we disguised you?"

"Do you mean like an actor or a thief? I thought faerie glamour didn't work anymore?" Navarre asked.

Galessel's eyes lit up. "Exactly that, Navarre. We can

use mortal theater techniques. I've been reading about it in some of the books Muriel brought back with her the last time she was in Arturia."

Clove grinned, and her ears twitched with excitement. "That gives me some ideas, too. Come on Galey. Let's go try something."

Clove and Galessel practically ran off toward the palace, leaving Navarre and Morgan alone.

"That was entertaining," Morgan said. "Do they do that often? Go running off without as much as a 'by your leave?'"

Navarre shrugged. "This is the first, though to be fair, Clove has not been around the palace much in this last year, as you know. Come, there's still tea back at the table. Tell me what's been happening out in the world."

⊛ ⊛ ⊛

"I'm more worried about what's not going on in Arturia than what is," Morgan said after taking a sip of tea. She had freshened up since the council with the elven king. Her cream cotton shirt and leather pants were free of the travel dust that streaked them earlier, and her red hair, now clean, sparkled in the sunlight, like fiery embers.

"Oh? What news have you? Messages from home have been few and far between lately." Navarre tipped back in his chair, balancing on two legs.

Morgan traced a swirl pattern in the wood of the table with her finger. "That's just it. We went by the Moon Gate to check for messages before coming here, and there were none. Clove's network has been quiet, too. Normally it would mean things are quiet, but with what we heard earlier, it worries me."

"What was the last you heard?"

"Victoria has pulled back some of her troops from garrisons in more compliant colonies and quiet borders. The loss of the stockpiled supplies hurt her, but word was she increased taxes on some of the colonies to make it up."

"We suspected she'd do as much." Navarre shrugged and tucked a stray dread back under his head scarf. "What of the social unrest?"

"The fae and lower class have banded together and are fighting to form labor unions and gain equal rights. So, the protests continue, but they're not as big as after the stockpiles of food and such were revealed. Victoria's people have done a decent job redirecting the story to blame corrupt officials."

Morgan threw one of her many daggers at a tree to her left. Her aim was true, and rings rippled out along the bark as if she'd thrown a stone into a pond. A discordant sound, like mismatched wind chimes, began to emanate from the tree. Morgan shot a worried look at Navarre before jumping up and retrieving her dagger. She whispered something to the tree, and the sound slowly faded. "Oops. Probably shouldn't have done that. Been here off and on for nearly a year, and I still can't get used to the idea that practically everything here is alive."

Navarre nodded. He was constantly surprised by things here. The gardens and grounds were wild enough. He couldn't imagine what it was like outside. The idea of having the freedom to explore this plane thrilled and terrified him.

"Speaking of magic," Morgan continued, 'they've done something ingenious in Arturia. A couple of druids from the enclave on the Isle of Mann heard about the plight of the fae and the poor in Ashelon. They found a way to create magic doorways into the tunnel system, and apparently even direct doors to places like Eire and Skotia, as emergency escape routes. The magic is keyed to fae blood and won't work for humans unless they have a charm."

Navarre stroked his short-cropped beard, his mind

spinning on the tactical implications of the escape routes. He regretted not being in Arturia to help plan the best locations or help with other logistics. "Hopefully they won't need them, but I'm glad those routes are in place.

"One thing troubles me, though: the charms. While I understand the need for charms for human allies, it leaves the potential for some desperate soul to sell one or have one stolen and used by Victoria's men."

Morgan nodded. "I thought of that, too, and apparently the druids did, as well. The humans have to swear a blood oath not to betray the fae or the locations of the doors when they receive the charm. Otherwise the charm won't work."

Navarre suppressed a shudder. He hated blood-based magic. It felt wrong somehow; a blood sacrifice, but one you could make over and over until you depleted yourself either physically, or spiritually, or both. Shuddering at the thought, he changed the subject.

"So, tell me about you and Samga. She doesn't strike me as someone who'd do casual relationships."

Morgan blushed, a rare thing for the cocky sharpshooter. "She doesn't. Her people are stubbornly monogamous." She shrugged and leaned back in her chair, draping an arm over the low back. "Being on the road so long together, I've really gotten to know her. Once you crack that silent warrior exterior, you find a deeply spiritual and amazingly funny person. She might just make an honest woman out of me."

Navarre laughed. "Is that even possible?" Morgan was a notorious womanizer, worse than any man he'd ever known. If she kept the same woman in her bed for more than a night, it was something to be remarked on.

Morgan turned serious, leaning forward and looking earnest. "No, I'm serious, Nav. I've never really been in love, you know that. Never wanted to be. It was more fun, and easier, to keep things casual. Especially in our line of business. But Samga, she's different. I feel better around her. Like the world is more right somehow." Morgan smiled. "I'm guessing you might know what that's like?"

It was Navarre's turn to blush. He tried to hide it behind his coffee mug. He couldn't help but smile when he thought of Galessel. "Maybe," he hedged.

Morgan huffed and leaned back again. She looked smug. "I knew it! I saw it back in Arturia. You couldn't keep your eyes off her, and back there, during the sparring match, that wasn't just the look of a proud mentor on your face." She laughed. "You're in love with her."

"Can you blame me? She's got a strength of will like no other—except maybe you." He smiled at his old friend. They'd tried courting a long time ago, but they were better friends and shield mates than lovers.

"It doesn't hurt she's got that ethereal elven beauty, either," Morgan teased.

"I'd love her even if she was a dwarf. She makes the world more right when she's around." Navarre's chest swelled with love just thinking about her. Galessel had been through hell and refused to be quelled by it. Her strength made him strive to be better himself.

"I'd tease you, but now I know myself. I'm happy for you." Morgan cocked her head, a glint in her eye. "So how's—"

"Hey! There you are." Clove came striding into the little garden enclosure. A white-haired woman followed close behind her. "I'd like to introduce you to Sasha, my personal bodyguard."

Sasha was tall and dressed in pants and a top that changed from blue to purple depending on the light. She wore a brown leather corset, belt, and bracers, with a hydronium pistol holstered at her hip.

Morgan smiled and nodded. Navarre stared. Sasha looked familiar.

Sasha's black lips moved into a smile, and her blue eyes sparkled. She tucked a strand of long hair behind a perfectly round ear.

It was the smile that finally did it for Navarre. "Galessel?"

"Sasha" laughed. "Took you long enough. I don't know if I should be pleased or insulted, Navarre." She spoke in a perfect Arturian accent. All hints of her elven lilt were gone.

Both Navarre and Morgan stood to get a better look at Galessel's disguise. It was good. Better than most theater makeup he'd seen. Her ears looked human with no sign of prosthetics. "How'd you cover your ears? They look perfect." He felt bad for saying it. He knew how sensitive she was about her ears.

Galessel actually smiled, though. "We used a mixture of sticky putty and kobi berry juice. That stuff takes days to wear off."

"It was simple enough after that to match her skin tone with stage makeup. A thin coat of strawfaerie juice to seal it, and she can weather a typhoon without it coming off," Clove added.

"And the eyes?" Morgan asked. "Those are different, too, right? Aren't they normally purple?"

Galessel blinked a couple of times. The whites of her eyes were a little red. "Pixie dust. That's temporary, though, and it itches. I might not be able to use it, but it was worth a try. Not many humans with purple eyes."

"Goggles or dark spectacles would disguise your eyes easily enough," Morgan offered. She walked around Galessel, taking in the new look. "Well done."

"I'm impressed with your accent. I didn't know you'd been practicing," Navarre said.

"I haven't been. I just told myself I could do it, and now I can!" She smiled and there was a hint of mischief in her eyes. "Pretty amazing, right?"

"Yeah. Amazing," Navarre and Morgan said together.

Clove looked at her friend, one ear cocked to the side.

Something wasn't quite right about Galessel's newfound ability to mimic an Arturian accent. It wasn't troublesome, but it was curious. However, it did tie the whole disguise together. Navarre was anxious to see if Galessel could fool her parents. If she could, they just might be able to get out of the palace.

STRAWFAERIE

Chapter 4
Alexandria

Murik guided *Death's Embrace* over the heavily forested island of Alexandria. The nearly full moon shone down, silvering the treetops and causing his ship to cast a wide shadow. The stars were faint, as if they feared to shine too brightly. In the distance, white marble single-story buildings appeared to glow in the moonlight. Small clearings, some with open-air structures, dotted the forest. Murik kept his eye on a larger space up ahead. He flipped a switch on the wall console to his left and began speaking.

"ETA: five minutes. Keep your weapons concealed at all times. You might not be able to see the centaurs, but rest assured they've already got their eyes on us." He flipped off the switch and began maneuvers to land the ship in the clearing.

Blood-bonding with a ship had its advantages. While his crew had been exceptional, being able to land *Death's Embrace* without the distraction of men yelling on deck was almost meditative. Murik could sense the slight crosscurrent in the air as the ship descended below the tops of the trees and was able to adjust the trim of the guide-sails almost immediately. He leveled out the buoyancy of the balloon and retracted the larger motors. In his mind's eye, he could see the ground and feel the ship's distance from it. A moment more of thought and the ship settled a precise five feet above the ground.

Murik flipped two switches in succession; a portion of the rail on the starboard side retracted and the gang plank lowered to the ground. Kane and his men began disembarking. Several at the back carried lead boxes between them.

Murik joined Kane and his men on the ground. The humans looked nervous. Many of them had hands in their pockets or under their coat jackets—gripping weapons, if he wasn't mistaken. Even Kane looked anxious. Stupid humans would get themselves killed before they fulfilled their usefulness if they weren't careful.

"Ease up, gentlemen." Murik tried to sound reassuring. He'd rather yell, but humans were so flighty, it'd only make things worse. "The centaurs are a neutral race. They won't hurt you if you don't do anything stupid first."

Several men glared at him, but most of them tried to relax their postures, and a few even pulled their hands out of their pockets. Good.

"Aren't the Svellvega the enemies of nearly everyone in the Hidden Lands?" Kane asked. He had been one who'd taken his hand out from under his jacket, but now his arms were crossed.

"Not everyone. We've converted quite a few of the fae to our side in recent months." Murik smiled. It was more of an upturn of one corner of his mouth, but it was as close as he ever got to smiling. "I have a centaur on the inside, as you would say. Zissis is a historian and agreed to take us into Alexandria proper in exchange for being the one who writes the epic about the rise of the Svellvega. Of course, he has no idea why we're really here."

Kane's eyes kept darting to the dark edges of the clearing. "That makes two of us. Why are we *here*, fly? You have yet to explain."

Murik ignored the derogatory slight and shook his head. He could hear hoof beats approaching. He grabbed Kane's elbow and guided him toward the east end of the clearing. "You'll see in due time. Have you ever met a centaur? I have to admit they are a bit imposing when you meet one for the first time."

A male centaur trotted into the clearing. He was small for a centaur, Murik noted, even though his human half still towered above the humans' heads by several feet. A loose white tunic, long enough to obscure the joining of man and horse, was draped over his torso and tied with a long leather belt at what would equate to his waist. His equine body was a dappled grey with a dark tail that would turn white with age.

If the centaur lived long enough. Murik suppressed a smirk.

The centaur slowed to a walk and then stopped just out of reach of the humans. He removed a leather-bound book and a quill from a satchel slung across his torso. He studied the group for a moment, then began writing. The humans started to grumble at being so soundly ignored. After a few pages of writing, the centaur closed his book and smiled.

"Murik, it pleases me to see you, but I was not expecting a large gathering. Who are your friends?" He prepared to write again.

Zissis's constant scribbling was annoying, but it was their ticket into Alexandria, so Murik tolerated it. He forced himself to smile in return. "Zissis, it pleases me to see you, as well. This is Kane and his students. They are scholars from Ashelon, and they are eager to learn about the magic of the greatest city in all of the Hidden Lands. I've told them all about your amazing library, and they wish to see it for themselves."

Zissis scribbled something quickly, then approached the group. Murik and Kane held their ground, but several of the other men took a few steps back. "I have never met a human before." He leaned forward, studying Kane, then quickly sketched something. He did this several times, before Kane finally lost his patience.

"We don't have a lot of time here, Mr. Zissis. If you would take us to the library, we would be obliged."

Murik was impressed by Kane's ability to sound annoyed yet polite at the same time. The nuance seemed to pass right by Zissis.

"Oh, yes. How rude of me. Come with me, and I'll show you the library and answer any questions you might have."

✸ ✸ ✸

Kane was unimpressed by the centaur city. It was too open and smelled like horses, obviously, though unlike the streets of Arturia, the thoroughfares in Alexandria were free of manure. So they were at least more civilized than horses. Not that it really mattered. In the dawn light, the buildings looked to all be of carved white marble. Many had no roof, and they were all a single story. As intelligent as they appeared, apparently they still hadn't mastered stairs.

Zissis rambled on like an enthusiastic tour guide, but Kane ignored most of it, keeping his ears open only for bits of tactical information and keeping an eye on Murik for clues of what was worth his attention. He also kept an eye on the crowd following them. The closer they got to the city center, the more centaurs joined the herd beginning to surround them. Good. The more the merrier for what was coming.

The library, once they finally got there, was huge— roughly four city blocks, if Kane gauged it right. It was still only a single story tall, like the surrounding buildings, and roofed with red slate tiles. The doors were huge metal behemoths with reliefs of all sorts of fairy creatures doing all sorts of things. Unlike places of learning in Arturia, they were not barred but stood wide open. Three centaurs abreast could easily pass through them, and three did as Kane's group approached.

The creatures stopped momentarily, nodded to Zissis, looked askance at the humans, and then kept walking. It baffled Kane as to why no one was questioning their presence here.

"Friend Murik, now that we are at the library, what topic interests you and your friends?"

Murik made a show of thinking before he replied. "The nature of magic. Specifically, witch lines and nodes."

This was all news to Kane, but he kept his mouth shut, knowing Murik had some plan yet and would give them the signal when it was time.

"Ah! A topic I have studied extensively in my search for the true the origin of the fae. Follow me!" Zissis all but pranced into the library, his hooves thudding on the packed dirt floor. He led them past rows and rows of leather-and-leaf bound books, walls lined with cubicles of scrolls, and then into a smaller wing of the building. The centaur stopped in front of a hundred-foot-long map, a mosaic of tiny tiles showing what Kane assumed was the entirety of the Hidden Lands. Black lines of some shiny stone crisscrossed the map like a mad spider's web. The lines, while haphazard at first glance, appeared to originate or terminate at one of five fist-sized garnets scattered across the map.

Zissis pointed to one, saying, "We're here, in Alexandria, one of the oldest nodes in the Hidden Lands. The only one older is at Vasyann, over there." He pointed to another garnet-marked spot on a small island at the far end of the map. "Witch lines, the principal channels of magical energy in the Hidden Lands, originate from fionnagh, or Mother Stones, and flow both above and below ground. Unfortunately, no one has been able to uncover the origin of fionnagh, but some scholars surmise all fae in the Hidden Lands owe our very existence to them. It is thought they anchor the original divine magic to this realm. I find that fascinating, as we all know the Great Goddess and her cohorts created us because they desired company and amusement in the vastness of the firmament."

Zissis paused, seeming to sense the boredom emanating from Kane's men. Kane could see a couple of them studying the map and eying the obviously precious stones making up many of the landmarks. Others looked around the library, pulling out various scrolls or thumbing through books written in a script they couldn't read. None of them were paying attention to Zissis.

Kane knew they were mentally mapping out exits and possible lines of attack should Murik decide this was the place. Kane hoped not. There weren't enough centaurs in the library proper. The herd that had followed them into the city center had disbursed when they entered the library.

Murik urged Zissis to continue, so the centaur resumed his lecture. "But that is not the question you asked, friend Murik, so I will not digress. Smaller nodes, or hex pools, are created by the crossing of a few witch lines, and in some cases have been manipulated into Moon Gates, which draw power from the lines to transport users from one gate to another. There's a fascinating story about the origins of the ancient war between the R'vikki and the D'zur—"

Murik cut the centaur off. "Zissis, while the tale of that war is no doubt interesting, I'd like to know more about the fionnagh. Could we see the one here? There isn't one in DawnGuard, my home, and in fact, no one but the centaurs seems to know where they all are."

"Oh, quite right. We've kept that knowledge alive here, along with things we've forgotten that we've forgotten." The centaur laughed but stopped abruptly when no one joined him. He gestured back toward the entrance. "Please, follow me. The fionnagh isn't far from here."

Kane pulled Murik aside while the rest of his men followed the centaur. "What's the plan? What exactly are you waiting for?"

Murik smiled. It wasn't a warm expression. "Zizzis is leading us to the objective. Blow up the fionnagh, and with any luck, we'll destroy the centaurs. And if I'm wrong, then we at least weaken the flow of magic through the Hidden Lands, and your men get to do some sport shooting." Murik looked toward the library entrance where Zissis was waiting. "Let's go. We wouldn't want to keep them waiting."

Zissis led them from the library and past an ornate courtyard of sculpted topiaries of creatures Kane had never seen before. Shapes of strange, long-necked, winged beasts looking like someone had smashed a giraffe and a duck together, were mixed in with other odd, impossible creatures.

Kane couldn't wait to burn it all down.

Their centaur guide led them toward a park-like area with a large circle of what looked like oak trees. Kane noticed everything looked a little lusher around a red stone pillar in the middle of the trees. Flowers bloomed at its base and delicate vines wound around it. As they got closer, Kane could make out faint carvings of centaurs and other horse-like creatures.

Zissis stopped before the stone and stood proudly. "This is the fionnagh of Alexandria. Isn't it beautiful?"

Kane and his men made appropriate appreciation noises. A pair of centaurs, one male, the other female, approached, and Zissis bowed deeply, folding a foreleg under as he bowed his head and put his right hand to his forehead. "Majesties, you honor us with your presence. I hope we did not disturb you?"

The male, whose horse body was a deep chestnut and whose torso was bare except for an expanse of dark hair on his chest, said, "Rise, Zissis, and introduce us to your guests." Sunlight flashed from a crown of gold on his head, which was partially obscured by long chestnut hair.

"Oh, yes, my apologies. I was so excited to take these esteemed scholars to the library that I neglected my duty to introduce them to you first." Zissis shifted nervously as he presented Murik and Kane and his men. "King Sophocles, Queen Savinna, may I present Murik—"

"Airship Captain—my home is in the skies," Murik interrupted. He bowed. "And this is Kane and his acolytes from Ashelon. Zissis was kind enough to invite us here so that the humans might learn more about magic."

Kane bowed, subtly waving for the rest of his men to do so. He could tell the time was close and did not want to blow their cover. "We are honored, majesties, to meet such esteemed persons on our visit. Zissis has been a very gracious host." Kane nearly choked on his words, but he'd spent enough time around his own queen to know what to say. He just hated having to say it to the fae.

Murik stepped forward and bowed again. "Majesties, please excuse me. I must return to my ship and ready it for our return to Ashelon."

"But you only just got here," the queen said. Clad in a turquoise tunic, belted with gold rope, she had pale blonde hair and a cream colored coat like a palomino. "We've never had human guests before. There is much I'm sure we could learn from you, as well."

Murik actually managed to look regretful when he said, "Apologies, your majesty, but the scholars are on a lengthy tour of the Hidden Lands, and I'm afraid our schedule is very tight." He nodded and turned away from the centaur royalty.

As he walked passed, he put a hand on Kane's shoulder and said, "Don't be too long in your study here. We depart in an hour."

When Murik was gone, the king walked toward Kane, and it was all Kane could do to not take a step back. Kane's head barely cleared the king's equine shoulders. The creature was huge!

"I am sorry your stay here will be so short. But tell me, what do your acolytes carry in those metal crates?"

Kane put on his best courtier act. "Ah, your majesties, though our time here is short, we brought gifts from the human realm. Please, take a look."

Kane's men put the crates down and opened them. One of the men tossed a grenade to Kane, who caught it and held it out to the King. The centaur stepped back a pace and held his hand to his head as if he were in pain. "Is that...cold-iron?"

"Yes, yes, it is, you dumb pony." Kane pulled the pin and threw the grenade at the fionnagh as he and his men ran toward the trees. The grenade exploded as they reached the cover of the giant trunks. The ground began to roll, and a rumble like a locomotive seemed to come from everywhere. Centaurs and men screamed. Kane pressed his back to the tree, wondering if Murik had betrayed them. Would destroying the fionnagh, destroy everything around it and not just the centaurs?

Kane's stomach rolled with the earth. He gripped the tree so hard his knuckles turned white. Several giant oaks fell during the shaking. When things settled down, Kane peeked around the cover of the tree to see the bodies of the king, queen, and Zissis surrounding the demolished fionnagh. The bodies of the dead centaurs were melting into goo.

Kane and his men gathered their weapons and several grenades each and started back to the center of the city. Their rapid-firing hydronium guns made short work of the centaurs they found screaming and wandering around in shock in the ruined streets. After several blocks, they heard what sounded like approaching cavalry. Taking up positions behind the rubble of a ruined building, they threw several grenades at what appeared to be royal guards.

Dressed in red livery and brandishing scimitars, the guards were not immune to cold-iron. The odd human-horse screams of the dying centaurs was music to Kane's ears—painful, but music nonetheless. Several of his men laughed as those centaurs not instantly killed by the grenades convulsed painfully before dissolving.

He and his men continued to cover their retreat with gunfire until they reached *Death's Embrace*, which Murick had moved to the entrance of the city.

The ruined marble gates, shattered and strewn like children's blocks, made a convenient stair to the airship. As soon as the last of Kane's men were aboard, Murik lifted off. Kane stayed near the rail but was forced to dodge a spear. He hunkered down behind an air intake on the deck after an arrow thunked into the wood of the rail where he'd just been.

After they'd gained altitude, Kane looked over the rail again. The city below, obscured by smoke and dust, lay in ruin. Everything still green quickly turned into dead grey before Kane's eyes, the devastation spreading out in rings around cold-iron remnants left behind by the grenades.

The cacophony of whinnies and cries from the surviving populace made Kane cover his ears. As much as he enjoyed the reasons behind the cries, he'd never liked the death screams of horses.

Abruptly all attacks upon the airship ceased.

Kane realized Murik had ceased to gain altitude. He wondered at that, until he realized Murik wanted to see what was going to happen. Kane kept watching, as well. The attack had gone better than he'd hoped.

And then something even better happened. The centaurs started disappearing! At first they turned ghostly, transparent. Confusion and horror apparent on their faces, even from this distance, their bodies dissipated into clouds of gold-hued sparkles that drifted into the spreading smoke and was lost. Soon, the city below was completely empty and as silent as a tomb. Not even a bird could be seen in the vicinity.

Kane's men cheered and he laughed. His lieutenant, Joe Hill, came over and stood at the rail with him. "I had no idea cold-iron would do that, boss."

"Honestly, I don't think cold-iron works that way, even here. I've seen it melt fae in Arturia or turn them to ash, but only if an individual had been hit. Some of those asses we never touched."

"It wasn't cold-iron that destroyed the centaurs," Murik said from behind them. Kane cursed himself for jumping but felt a little better because Joe did, too. He turned to face the cursed elf.

"What do you mean?"

"Were you paying attention when Zissis was talking in the library? Those old legends about the fionnagh being the reason the fae exist? We just verified them. The centaurs are gone because we destroyed their fionnagh. And the land here will be dead and poisoned for generations. If we destroy the other four fionnagh, we'll cripple the Hidden Lands."

Kane was ecstatic at the news. Victoria would knight him when he returned. But something bothered him. "If these stones really are the lifeblood of the fae here, won't destroying all of them kill you, too?"

"Why would I care?" Murik replied. The blue tinge to his face got darker. "I'm a half-breed. Rejected by my father, then sold into slavery, no one gave a half-dral about me. I want to watch this place burn."

Kane exchanged a glance with Joe, who shrugged. Maybe this would be a suicide mission after all. Not exactly what Kane had planned. Not to mention it put Murik's stability in question. A man who didn't care if he lived or died wouldn't care about their lives either. On the other hand, if Murik gave them a way to completely destroy the Hidden Lands, they'd be honored as heroes—alive or dead.

Kane shrugged, accepting the risk. "All right. I think we can make that happen. We've got a gun in the hold that will fire a cold-iron bomb the size of a crate. But we only have one. And that's meant for Soji."

Murik smiled, and it gave Kane the chills. "That's perfect. After seeing the centaurs' map, I think I know where the vile creature is. It won't know what hit it."

Kane wondered if the bomb would leave enough of the creature for him to bring home a trophy. What a prize that would be. "Well, what are we waiting for? Let's go."

Murik shook his head. "Not quite yet. We need to take out a few more fionnagh first. After what happened today, the other races will be on their guard. I'll need to drop in fast, off-load your men and take off again."

Kane didn't like the sound of that and said so. "And what's to keep you from stranding us?"

"If I'm not dead, I'll come back for you. If I am, your men can do whatever they want until your Queen sends in her army. Either way, you've won." He smirked and headed back to the ship's control room.

For the second time that day, Kane suppressed a shudder. The things he did for his queen.

Chapter 5
Near Avondale

Queen Kaneti tucked a stray glacial-blue and black braid behind her pointed ear with one hand, while the other hand kept the glowing map of the Hidden Lands floating above the blackwood table in the center of her war tent. A black pillar marked the Anisbarii palace, while to the northeast, along the coast near Avondale, several neat rows of blue flame flickered, representing her and her Svellvegan army. Her four most trusted generals stood around the table, and a handful of minor aides and lieutenants lined the flat white walls. All of them had their furs draped over an arm. It was too warm so far south of DawnGuard.

Even Kaneti had discarded her royal furs. Her black fur cape sat piled, forgotten, in a corner, and her blood red robes were darkened with sweat.

"Your Excellency, how long before Davorin brings his human pets to heel and starts his attacks?" asked Bashuru, the most senior of her generals, and the only one with earrings even close in size to her own. His lobes hung low, stretched by the weight of the golden rings.

"He should be here by now," Kaneti said, doing her best to keep from growling. "My spies saw Murik's ship pass through the Sun Gate near Alexandria this morning."

Kaneti would have said more, but she felt a vibration pass through the thick leather soles of her boots, and she was overcome with vertigo, causing her map illusion to flicker. At the same time, a thunder-like rumbling began to build in volume, growing all around them.

And then the world tumbled.

The map disappeared as the ground beneath them rolled and buckled. The rumbling rose to a deafening level. Moon crystal lamps toppled, casting chaotic shadows that pulsed with the rolling turf. Her generals, arms akimbo, succumbed to the shaking earth, falling to their knees. Kaneti, determined to keep her footing, managed it only for a few moments before she, too, fell.

After a time, the rumble faded and the world quit shaking. The frightened and pained screams of elves, nightsteeds, and others, however, continued.

Bashuru held out a hand, and Kaneti took it just long enough to gain her feet. Without a word, she pushed her way past fallen aides and out into the chaos of what had been a very orderly war camp. The army's conical white tents lay in heaps, torn and tangled among toppled weapons racks. Blocks of earth jutted from the ground in places, and large cracks gaped in others. Across the way, a pair of nightsteeds stomped out the flames on a downed tent which had fallen into a cook fire, and the faint cacophony of redcaps arguing came from further in the camp. Elves and beasts were regaining their feet, but no one appeared to be seriously hurt.

Behind her, speculation began about what had happened, her generals surmising this must have been some sort of Anisbarii weapon. The earth didn't shake in the Hidden Lands. But something felt off to Kaneti—she just couldn't put a dagger in it.

The violent shaking of a nearby nightsteed caught her eye just as the creature started screaming. His skin rippled along dark flanks as his face contorted in pain. Kaneti watched in fascination as the nightsteed, a lead in her cavalry judging by the blue rank tattoos on his biceps, started to give off black sparks and slowly, painfully faded from view. Within the span of an ancient dragon's heartbeat, the screaming stopped. Every nightsteed had vanished in a cloud of glowing red hooves and black sparks as if the fiery pits of the demon realm had finally claimed them.

"Cowards! Asher-blasted beasts ran at the first sign of trouble. I knew we couldn't trust them." Ziurdath huffed. Kaneti's general-sagittarii was so angry his skin had turned dark blue. He'd been reluctant to bring the nightsteeds into the ranks of his archers, having little respect for anything but his own people, but aside from their light-kin, the centaurs, they were—or had been—the best archers in the Hidden Lands. Ordering him to include them had been one of the few good things Kaneti's fool of a husband had actually done in recent memory.

"Have you ever seen a nightsteed run from anything, Ziurdath?" Shirdre chided. The female illusionist, Kaneti's closest aide, turned up her petite nose at the general. "It was obviously some new magic concocted by the Anisbarii. Though how they managed to make an entire race disappear without using the darker arts is beyond my reckoning." Shirdre had recently received the final cheek tattoos—black curved dagger-like markings, that together with the black dots above her eyebrows, marked her as a master. But she still didn't know everything.

Only a few ever received the chin line as Kaneti had. Flowing from her lower lip, the line broke into shorter and shorter segments until it disappeared above the hollow of her throat. It was that extra level of mastery that told the Svellvega queen this was neither a desertion nor Anisbarii magic, but frustratingly, it also didn't tell her what had happened.

"Enough!" Kaneti commanded. The chatter and speculation died immediately. "Generals, see to your troops. Get this camp back in order. We'll reconvene in an hour. Bring me useful information only." Her generals and their aides bowed deeply and hurried away.

Kaneti stormed back into her tent. The guard at the entrance barely got the door open for her fast enough. Shirdre followed her in. No others would dare without an express invitation. She could feel the illusionist trembling behind her and almost turned to slap her, but she thought better of it. It was by force of will alone that Kaneti held her own shaking in check. What had happened was unprecedented. Something was very wrong. It disturbed her she didn't know what it was.

"Shirdre, find the redcap scouts and send two into the Anisbarii lands. I want to know if this was a weapon or something more dire."

"Yes, my queen." Shirdre bowed nearly in half and left the tent on silent feet.

Finally alone, Kaneti drew a shuddering breath, then another, smoother, one. When she'd calmed her heartbeat, she moved her hands through the familiar forms to conjure a map of the Hidden Lands. Nothing happened. The simple spell would not activate. She tried again, but nothing appeared above the blackwood table. She tried several more spells, like turning the tent green, and conjuring her own image before her, but nothing worked. Only the simplest spell all young females know instinctively worked; making her skin appear pale and sickly like an Anisbarii.

Asher blast it! Had the Anisbarii found a way to block her magic?

The rushing sound of flames, and a wave of heat at her back, stopped her runaway thoughts. Before she even turned around, she knew what she'd see: Asher, god of chaos and leader of the new black trinity of gods.

He stood with black flames licking at his feet. His red robes accented his grey skin and hugged a muscular form the envy of even the strongest Svellvega. Though the robes flowed to the floor, they were immune to the corrupt flames.

Kaneti bowed low before his glowing orange eyes could catch her own.

"You called, my dear?" Asher's voice was spun honey and spite. It gave Kaneti chills that both thrilled and scared her. She rose from her bow but kept her eyes on the triangle of bare chest above the crossed fabric of his robe.

"My lord. In my frustration, it appears I did. Please forgive my arrogance."

The god waved away the apology, draping himself across her blackwood throne. Intricately carved out of a single tree, the chair was both delicate and imposing. Kaneti couldn't help but look to see if Asher's black flames were affecting her favorite piece of furniture. To her relief they appeared to be just an illusion. "Lord, what has happened? Why does everything but the simplest illusion fail?"

Asher raised an eyebrow. "I'm afraid, my darling queen, the females of your kind have been reduced to casting personal illusions." He shrugged and picked something from beneath a pointed black fingernail.

Kaneti's entire being was focused on illusion, and now her god had taken that away? She'd worked too hard, sacrificed her own blood, to get where she was at. She wasn't about to lose all that to a fickle god. "How dare you! Svellvegan females have worshiped you for centuries, and this is how you repay our reverence?" She forgot herself and looked him in the eyes.

Dark vortexes of chaos pulled at Kaneti's soul. She couldn't breathe, couldn't move. She was drowning.

Asher blinked, freeing Kaneti. He smiled, and Kaneti immediately dropped her gaze , falling to one knee. Her god began to laugh. "Ah, Kaneti. I enjoy your rage. It's like the fires of my own heart. But this bit of chaos is not my doing." His voice deepened and the heat of his flames intensified. "It was one of you, the one you call Murik. We gods are not amused. If we—if I—wanted the Hidden Lands destroyed, I'd do it myself!"

Kaneti raised her head but did not look Asher in the eye again. "Then I will send out my army to scour this land

and find this traitor. I will bring him to you in flames."

The heat from Asher intensified and Kaneti shrank back.

"No, my dear Kaneti, you will not."

The god's statement took her aback, but he didn't give her space to ask why.

"Murik is someone else's fate. Donnan has other plans for you."

Asher's fire rose around him with a rush of heat, and then he was gone.

Kaneti waited a few breaths before rising and slumping down on her throne. It was hot and likely burnt, but that wasn't important anymore.

What did Asher mean that Donnan had other plans for her? It wasn't every day one learned they were a pawn in a god's game. Dealing with this war was bad enough.

This war. Tension suffused Kaneti's entire body. Cursing Davorin, she stood and started pacing. She wouldn't be stuck out here in this gods-blasted heat if it wasn't for him and his hare-brained scheme. Where was he? Davorin was supposed to have been back with that half-breed Murik this morning. Did the humans betray them, or did they betray her?

She couldn't trust any of them. She shoved over a silver candle stand in frustration. Unlit candles scattered across the tent floor. Even the light lasted too long here!

Davorin wanted to soften up the Anisbarii with small skirmishes, then bring fifty thousand human soldiers into the Hidden Lands. It was pure madness. What was to stop the humans from slaughtering all of them and taking over themselves? Nothing, that's what. Especially now that her nightsteed cavalry had vanished in a puff of sparks. Five thousand highly trained soldiers just gone.

Her husband thought Davorin was brilliant, the way he snuggled up to the human queen, Victoria. Out of all the humans Kaneti had ever met, Queen Victoria was the worst—she'd betray Davorin in a hummingbird's heartbeat, and none of the males around Kaneti could see it. Her stupid husband had gone along with Davorin's plan, and so here she was.

This whole endeavor was a lost cause. Depending upon the humans to help the Svellvega achieve dominance in the Hidden Lands had been a mistake from the beginning. Kaneti stopped pacing as the solution solidified in her mind. She had one chance to make this right and make sure her people would survive the stupidity of her fool of a husband and that fop Davorin.

Later that evening, Kaneti's redcap scouts returned. The two diminutive fae held their pointed, blood red hats in their hands and kept their eyes on the ground as they gave their report.

"Highness, we scoured the camp and the area beyond. The nightsteeds are gone, but whatever happened, they didn't go willingly. Witnesses say they all appeared to be in horrible pain, and many appeared to struggle against what was happening to them, as if they knew they were destined for Freyka's grey halls."

"And the cause?"

The redcaps clutched their hats tighter and bowed lower. The one with the beard that reached to his pointed metal boots said, "Oh, gracious majesty, no one knows. No Anisbarii have been seen in the area at all, and a returning airship scout reported there are no visible long-range weapons on their borders."

No Anisbarii nearby meant they likely weren't to blame for all this. So who was? Kaneti would have to meditate on it. "Very well. That matter requires more investigation, but there is something else I'd like you to do now. Take the Moon Gate to DawnGuard and deliver a *final* message to my husband, the king."

The bloodthirsty fae grinned wickedly, showing their shark-like teeth, and bowed. "It shall be done your majesty." They practically ran out of the tent in their excitement.

Alone again in her tent, Queen Kaneti quietly noted to herself, "He has outlived his usefulness. Actually, he's been useless since our daughter was conceived. The Svellvega cannot survive much longer on raids, war, and thievery. And they certainly don't need the help of humans. It's time for the Svellvega to flock to my banner now. And forever."

Chapter 6
Anisbar

Galessel entered her father's strategy room, doing her best to imitate Morgan's walk, swaying her hips and all but stomping her feet, all to appear more human. The odd looks directed her way could have been for any number of things: a strange human in the room, her odd gate, or even the fact everyone could see through her disguise. Regardless, she hoped she didn't look as unbalanced as she felt. The disguise might not be the best idea after all. The goji berry juice they used to keep the putty on her ears itched, and it took all her willpower not to reach for her ears.

She and Clove approached the king and queen standing off to one side. Her parents both eyed her suspiciously.

"Your majesties, may I introduce Sasha, an associate of mine from Ashelon. She has agreed to serve as my bodyguard during our next mission."

Galessel bowed. In her perfect human accent she said, "It's an honor your majesties. I am here to serve."

Queen Thessalia appraised her before addressing Clove. "I hardly think you need a bodyguard, Clove, but given the changing events, perhaps it is warranted." She looked around the room, her eyes briefly resting on Sasha. "Where is my daughter?"

Clove's ears twitched. "I'm afraid she's not feeling well, your majesty, and has decided to rest in her rooms. I promised to brief her once we're done."

Thessalia cocked an eyebrow at Clove and moved aside to let her pass farther into the room. As Galessel followed, her mother brushed her elbow and whispered, "I don't know what you're up to, daughter, but I trust you have a good explanation for your, uh, appearance."

Galessel cursed inwardly. Had Morgan and Navarre merely humored her when they said they couldn't tell it was her? Only one way to know. "How did you know, Mother?" she whispered back.

"I carried you in my belly for two years. I would know the energy field of my own daughter on the darkest of moonless nights." Thessalia smiled the half smile that Galessel knew meant she was amused but also worried. She'd seen that same look when she'd told her mother how she planned to arbitrate a dispute between the brownies and naiads at the beginning of her diplomatic career.

"We will discuss this after the meeting," her mother said. "Go. Stand with your friends. And remember your place as Clove's bodyguard. You are to be seen and not heard."

Galessel did as she was bid, cringing inside at her mother's admonition. She wasn't wrong. As a bodyguard, she should say nothing and see everything. Damn. Maybe she could whisper things for Clove to ask or comment on, assuming she wouldn't already.

She took her place just behind Clove's left shoulder at the large strategy table. Navarre was to Clove's left, and Morgan to his. Her father stood at one end, and several generals and advisors lined the other side of the table. Her mother took her place on the king's right side. On the table itself, a map of the Hidden Lands was laid out, with each of the races' territories delineated. Crescent shapes marked the Moon Gates, and several carved wooden ice bears, representing the Svellvega, were grouped near the coast of Avondale, the home of the hill giants. Twice as many carved unicorns were arrayed around a stone castle set to mark Anisbar's location on the map.

Her father looked worried. Everyone in the room did. The earthquake that had prompted this meeting was incredibly unusual. "I know everyone's been speculating on the cause of the earthquake, and we'll get to that shortly. But before we do, I want a report of the damage it caused and any casualties. Architect Emmyth, what do you know so far as to the extent of any damage?"

The aged architect moved through the group surrounding the table. He pointed to the central palace on the map with a short staff he used for walking. "The main palace doesn't seem to have sustained any significant damage. A few of the older decorative pieces have crumbled, but the building and surrounding structures are sound. It would take something four times as strong and much closer to do any damage. Initial reports from the city say there is only minor damage to some buildings. Nothing that can't be repaired in a few days' time." The grey-haired elf bowed from the shoulders and melted back into the crowd.

King Valandil nodded his thanks. "General Ilvisar, your casualty report."

Ilvisar turned toward the king, his hands concealed in his sleeves. "Majesties. Only minor injuries to report, caused by falling debris. Our adversity responders have extinguished several small fires, as well."

"Thank you, General. That is good news. I hope reports from the farther edges of our kingdom are as positive." He paused for a deep breath. "Let's discuss the possible cause. I know many immediately came to the conclusion the Svellvega were responsible, and that was also my first thought. But remember, their magics are purely illusion. Illusion can't cause the very real damage and injuries reported."

Valandil nodded to Navarre, who had raised his hand to shoulder level to get the king's attention.

"What about weapons? Could they have something capable of causing that kind of damage? We know they're encamped only a few hours from here by airship."

Galessel had seen this particular look of concentration on Navarre's face before and knew he was running a variety of scenarios through his mind.

Ilvisar responded. "It is possible. Reports from the epicenter have not yet come in. I'm afraid anything we may come up with is purely speculation at this point in time."

One of her father's other generals, one she did not know well, leaned forward. "The human brings up a good point."

"The human has a name," Clove interrupted. Her ears laid back in annoyance.

The general dipped his head to Navarre. "Forgive me, Navarre. I meant no disrespect." He turned his attention back to the map. "Navarre has a point. The Svellvega have a foothold on our land. Why are we not attacking? We easily outnumber them by at least two to one. More, if we can convince the Oak-kin to join in."

"The Oak-kin won't join us unless the Svellvega invade their forest," Clove noted. "But if they stray into the R'vikki's territory, those feisty felines will drop their neutrality and fight with us, at least long enough to rid their homeland of those poor excuse for elves."

"The Svellvega could just be a diversion." Galessel's mother didn't hide the contempt in her voice. "Something to keep us occupied while the humans from Ashelon sneak in. We must be vigilant for the human invasion." Galessel was just about to whisper a thought to Clove about recruiting the brownies as scouts when a breathless soldier ran into the room. His eyes were wide with shock, and the blue tunic and leather doublet marking him as an archer were covered in sparkling ash. He frantically looked around the room, and when he found the king and queen, he dropped to one knee facing them. Still gasping for breath, he said, "Majesties, they're gone! The centaurs are gone!"

Thessalia went to the archer and pulled him to his feet. "Calm yourself. Do you mean they fled?"

"No majesty. I—I—they started screaming after the earthquake and then they—they crumbled into ash! All of the centaurs are just—gone." The archer shook and his face went grey.

"Get this man a chair," Galessel's mother ordered.

Morgan got one under the archer just as he collapsed. His skin was ashen and covered in a sheen of sweat. "That was close," Morgan said. She checked the archer's pulse then addressed the queen. "Majesty, this man is in shock. He needs a physician."

Thessalia, her face a mask of concern, motioned for two guards in the back of the room to take the archer away. As they carried the elf out, the room burst into a cacophony of voices. Everyone was talking at once.

Everyone but Galessel.

She stared at the open doorway, trying to process what the archer had said. How could the centaurs have crumbled to ash? No race in the Hidden Lands had that kind of power. Except maybe Soji, if the legends were true, but the archer hadn't mentioned seeing the storied gryphon.

Galessel watched one of the generals leave the room, no doubt on a mission to learn more about what had just been reported. He stopped just outside the doorway, stepped back out of the way, and bowed. Queen Mother Annalinde slipped into the room, shaking her head at the general when he turned to announce her. He raised an eyebrow, then bowed and hurried out of the room.

Galessel's grandmother silently surveyed the room. Her eyes widened when they settled on Galessel. After a brief moment, she smiled softly and winked. Her mirth evaporated as she approached the table.

Everyone in the room was so preoccupied they didn't notice the elder elf until she put an age-spotted hand on her daughter's shoulder and gently moved her aside.

The elder queen's sudden appearance caused everyone to fall silent. She took advantage of the moment and said, "I know what happened."

No one said anything in response, waiting to hear what she had to say.

"How many of you know anything of fionnagh?"

The room stayed silent as those around the table only shook their heads.

"Time is short, but in deference to our human friends, I will explain enough for everyone to understand. We all know the gods created the Hidden Lands and every living thing here using their magic. But magic is fleeting and must return to its source, which means that the Hidden Lands and everything in it would have quickly disappeared without intervention. So, the gods created a way for magic to remain here permanently.

"Magic flows through the Hidden Lands like a network of rivers. You know these as Witch Lines. They flow in every direction—above and below ground. It is this magic that is responsible for the eternal springtime we enjoy. It is why we feel better here than in Ashelon, why we heal quickly and rarely become ill, and why we have longer life spans than the humans." Annalinde paused and looked around the table, making sure she still had everyone's attention. Navarre and Morgan appeared riveted by the elder queen's story. Galessel belatedly tried to mirror their expressions.

"Where two or more lines cross, a nexus is created which we call a Hex Pool. Silly name, but an ancient one. Probably named by some old Druid. But I digress." Annalinde waved away the thought like an annoying strawfaerie. "Magic tends to pool in these locations, and they are widely thought to be responsible for powering the barriers that exist between here and the mortal realm, the land of the dead, and even the Dreaming.

"There are places where six or more lines cross. These places are exceptionally powerful, and at each location is a physical marker called a fionnagh. Scholars through the ages have debated whether the lines originate from the fionnagh or if they are simply where many lines cross. What they do seem to agree upon is that these places are the anchor points of magic in the Hidden Lands. Without them, our magic would dissipate, and us along with it."

Everyone around the table was silent. Galessel looked at her mother, who'd gone pale as a unicorn's horn. After a moment, the queen spoke, "So what exactly are you saying, Mother?"

Annalinde let her gaze rest on each person before she said, "I'm saying exactly what you don't want to hear. The fionnagh in Alexandria has been destroyed. The centaurs and nightsteeds are gone." Her voice broke just a little. "No one ever imagined the fionnagh could even be damaged, let alone destroyed. If another one is destroyed, more races will disappear, and if they're all destroyed, the rest of the fae and the Hidden Lands will be no more."

There was a collective intake of breath, and everyone started talking at once again. And again, Galessel felt at a loss. She'd never heard of fionnagh, much less knew of their significance. Maybe it was because of their significance the knowledge was hidden.

"Grand—uh, Queen Annalinde, how do you know all this?" Galessel asked, hoping no one had heard her slip. Her mother shot her a look. Apparently she had.

"Child, I've been alive longer than many countries have been in existence in the mortal realm. Trust that I have done my fair share of studying, especially since my retirement from court," Annalinde chided.

Valandil silenced everyone in the room with a raised hand. "We need to find out how the fionnagh was destroyed and by whom." His gaze fell on Clove. "Clove, take Navarre and his people and a cadre of soldiers to

Alexandria via the Moon Gate. We need to get to the bottom of this new threat."

Clove nodded. "Yes, your majesty. We'll leave right away."

Annalinde stopped Clove with a hand on her arm. "The Moon Gate symbol to Alexandria has been burned out. You'll have to find another way."

"What do you mean burned out? How do you know?" Ilvisar's face was red—with anger or fear, Galessel couldn't tell. Their world had been completely upended. She wouldn't blame him if it was both.

"When I felt the disruption in the flow of the lines, I sent a page to check our Moon Gate. She reported that the symbol to Alexandria has blackened and is no longer whole."

Clove returned to the table and studied the map. "We can take the Moon Gate to Seya, assuming it's not damaged." She cocked an ear toward the queen mother, who shook her head. Clove continued, "N'hena's docked there. She can take us to Alexandria. It would be good to have the firepower of *The Intrepid*, just in case."

Valandil nodded his approval and the council disbursed in a somber silence.

Galessel remembered her place and preceded Clove out of the room, stopping just outside the door to let her friend pass. How her father hadn't uncovered her ruse, she didn't know. Why her mother was letting her go was an even deeper mystery, but she wasn't going to question her luck. She was finally getting out of the palace. She just wished it wasn't because of something so dire.

FIONNAGH
"One thing that Fae scholars all agree on is that the fionnagh, and there are a few, are the anchor points of magic in the Hidden Lands. Without them, our magic would dissipate, and us along with it."

Chapter 7
Alexandria

Navarre watched Clove elbow Galessel in the ribs as they sat at the small table. In the gathering room on *The Intrepid* the two sparred over a game of *Donerré*, an elven game of flattened engraved sticks Navarre likened to the human game of pinochle. "I do good work," the faun commented.

"Yes, you do. But I guess there's no fooling my mother or grandmother. They saw through the disguise right away," Galessel replied. Her eyes sparkled.

Navarre loved that look in her eyes, and at the moment, it was the only thing he recognized about her. The disguise Galessel and Clove had come up with really was that good. It was disconcerting to hear her voice and not see the face he'd come to love. He found it remarkable how changing her ears and hair could so completely transform her.

Clove held up her hand, fingers curled into a loose fist. "High hoof!"

Galessel giggled and mimicked Clove's hand with her own. They bumped fists and fell into a fit of laughter. Navarre couldn't help himself and joined in.

They all fell silent at the sound of a chime over the ship-wide sound system.

"Clove, Navarre, I think you and your team need to come out here. We're approaching Alexandria." Even through the tinniness of the sound system, N'hena Nikia, *The Intrepid*'s sylph captain sounded worried.

Chairs scraped along the wooden deck as they stood from the gaming table.

"Ladies," Navarre motioned with his hand for the women to go first through the double doors and out onto the main deck.

❀ ❀ ❀

The Intrepid touched down on the outskirts of Alexandria, near the remains of the city's gate. Most of the ship's crew, along with Navarre, Galessel and the others had looked down on the ruins of the city as they'd passed overhead. Navarre had never heard a ship's crew go so quiet.

The near total devastation was shocking. Navarre had expected to see centaur bodies, but here, too, they seemed to have vanished into the aether. Had he not known better, he'd have suspected the city to be ages dead, not mere days.

He led their group down the gangplank, his rapier at the ready. What struck him immediately was the lack of sound. There were no birds, no buzzing insects, no sounds coming from the forest behind them. Or what was left of it. The plants around the city were either dead or dying, wilting as if they'd been sprayed with poison.

Morgan, just behind him on his left as always, whispered, "I don't like this, Nav. The destruction is like nothing I've seen. And forgive me for saying this, but seeing bodies would make it a little less creepy."

Navarre nodded, his gaze sweeping the ruined gates for hidden soldiers and the nearby rooftops for snipers.

The lack of any living thing sent shivers down his back. He motioned them forward.

"Navarre!" Galessel called to him. Her voice sounded strained. He turned around and found her and Clove leaning against each other. Both women looked decidedly ill. There was a green cast to their features, which was saying something considering Clove's skin was covered in fine fur.

He rushed to them, noting all the fae who had disembarked looked ill. "What is it? What's wrong?"

Clove looked up at him. "Cold-iron poisoning. Has to be." The faun crumpled to the ground, taking Galessel with her.

Navarre picked up Clove, while Morgan helped Galessel stand. "Back to the ship. Now!" he yelled.

It took Navarre, Samga, and Morgan several trips to get everyone back on *The Intrepid*. There was visible improvement in the fae once they no longer touched the ground, but all still looked ill. Even N'hena's wings were looking grey though she hadn't set foot on the ground.

"Captain," Navarre said, "Samga, Morgan, and I will go into the city and investigate, as we are immune to the effects of the cold-iron. Get *The Intrepid* airborne again once we've disembarked and wait for us at a safe distance. We'll be back as soon as we can."

N'hena nodded and started barking orders to her crew.

Galessel put a hand on Navarre's arm. "Be careful. Cold-iron means Hammer Guardians. This could be a trap."

Navarre took her hand and kissed it. "*Ma chérie*, I am always careful, but I will be more so in order that I may return to you. I promise."

In fact, he wanted nothing more than to run into a few Hammer Guardians right now. Their bigotry at home was bad enough, but to come to a foreign land and commit genocide? He wanted to skewer the whole lot of them.

Taking the map of the city from Clove, he, Morgan, and Samga headed back into the city. The path into the heart of the centaur's capitol was not a straight one. Buckled earth left large blocks at odd angles, forcing the group to navigate around large cracks and collapsed buildings. The shadow of *The Intrepid,* following them from above, cast the ruined streets in a shroud of mourning.

It reminded Navarre of the ancient ruins of Rome, if Rome had fallen in a day. Occasionally, they would see bullet holes in the facades and statues. Samga scouted ahead but always came back with the same report. Nothing but rubble ahead.

They passed by what the map indicated was the main library. The large doors had toppled, and wisps of smoke still curled up from several places inside the expansive building. Peering in, Navarre noted some books had survived the fire. Not all of the centaurs' knowledge had been lost.

Sunlight shining in through collapsed sections of the roof sent smoky beams through the library, a pointed indication the knowledge wouldn't stay intact if it rained. He made a mental note to remember to tell Galessel when he returned. Someone would have to return soon to rescue the books.

Samga interrupted his thoughts. "Navarre, I believe I have found the remains of the fionnagh." The stoic archer's face was pale.

"Have you found bodies at last?" he asked, hoping that was the only cause of her distress.

She shook her head. "No. Still nothing. This city is void of everything, even ghosts."

He motioned for her to lead the way. Morgan fell into step beside him.

"It had to be a hit and run," she said. "Get in, destroy the fionnagh, get out. From what I can see, they might have had twenty men, maybe less. What I can't figure out is how they knew about the effects of destroying such a monument."

Navarre shrugged his shoulders. "Maybe we will know more when we see the thing ourselves, *mon amie.*"

As Samga led them farther down the main road, it became harder and harder to navigate the destruction. The earth had been completely tossed, as if a giant plow had broken the ground in haphazard rows, uprooting trees and reducing buildings to piles of rock.

They neared what might have once been a park. Giant oak trees had been turned to kindling, and everything was lying in a radial pattern, as if it'd been blown outward by a bomb.

Samga pointed to the center of the blast, where the remains of a pedestal stood, blackened and ruined. Navarre approached, but noted that Samga and Morgan moved to investigate the ruined giant trees. He pulled a drawing of the intact fionnagh from his breast pocket for comparison.

Galessel's grandmother had sketched it quickly, but even her sketch looked more alive than what stood before him. The fionnagh had once been very much alive or at least looked like it. In the drawing, a vine-covered pillar grew from the ground to embrace a crystal ball at its pinnacle, held in the petals of a flower. Now, it was a blackened stump. Dark ash lines marked where the vines had once been, and a sizable chunk was missing from one side. The shattered remains of the crystal sphere lay around the pillar, dull and abraded like the piece of beach glass he'd found on the beach near Cherbourg as a child.

He took stock of the lay of the destruction around the fionnagh. His initial assessment that it had to have been a bomb held true. Debris radiated out in a circular pattern from the fionnagh. He turned, surveying the park, and wondered at the size of bomb needed to be to topple such large trees. Or was it the destruction of the monument itself that caused all the damage? He had no measure of what this type of magic could actually do.

"Nav! You need to see this," Morgan called from near a tree to his left. Her voice sounded shaky. With anger or sadness, he wasn't sure.

As he approached, she held out something dull and grey to him. He couldn't make out what it was until he took it from her fingers. The thick concave piece of cast iron was part of a grenade. He looked up at Morgan, then around the park again. "How many fragments have you found?"

"Not many. One, maybe two grenades' worth?"

"And probably filled with powered cold-iron," Samga said. "Look at the ground. I thought it was ash and dead material making it look grey, but it's not. I tested it on my tongue. It's iron." A tear ran down Samga's cheek. "They wanted everything here to die, so they made sure it would by dusting it all with poison. A poison they are immune to."

"Damn Queen Victoria to all the hells!" Morgan's face was red and she was shaking. "This is what that bitch wanted for my people, for the Erien, but we were lucky. She didn't have a weapon like this, and we fought her off. This—this is genocide."

Navarre drew both women to him, putting his arms around them. He held back his own tears, converting them to rage, even as theirs flowed. He'd served Victoria faithfully for most of his life, leading her wars and subjugating foreign lands. The blinders had been pulled from his eyes years ago, but this made him truly hate his queen.

Samga pulled away first, never letting go of Morgan's hand. Morgan left Navarre's embrace then wiped the tears from Samga's face with her free hand.

"We will not let this stand unpunished, Morgan," Samga said. "We will avenge the centaurs and fight back, just as your people did."

Morgan half-smiled at her lover. "Yes, we will. We will make that bitch pay."

❂　❂　❂

On board *The Intrepid*, Galessel, along with the rest of the fae contingent, waited anxiously for Navarre, Samga, and Morgan's return. N'hena had only followed them for a short while. The closer they got to the city center, the worse everyone had felt. Everyone who'd fallen ill had recovered once the airship had returned to the outskirts of the city, but many reported a lingering fatigue. Eirsal remained below decks. His previous exposure to cold-iron somehow made him more susceptible to the poison and he was slow to recover.

Galessel had completely forgotten to maintain her ruse when she'd fallen ill, but luckily, everyone had been so preoccupied with aiding those who were ill that none seemed to notice that one of the humans had also been sick.

Galessel stood at the rail looking over the ruins of Alexandria while Clove and N'hena discussed the situation. It was all she could do to stay quiet and act her part as the two chatted.

"I wasn't sure I believed what you'd told me when you boarded, Clove, but I can't deny this." The sylph captain gestured sweepingly across the ruined scene. "Why would humans do this?"

"This is all Victoria and the Hammer Guardians' doing," Clove said. "Victoria wants the Hidden Lands' resources, and the Hammer Guardians hate everything fae. It's the perfect marriage of greed and bigotry." Clove's tawny ears drooped. "What I don't understand is how the Svellvega, even as much as they hate the rest of us, would sanction the destruction of the fionnagh."

N'hena shrugged. "Since when has anything the Svellvega have done made sense?"

The three of them stood in silence for several minutes. Galessel turned N'hena's question over in her mind but couldn't come to any better conclusion than the sylph had.

"Gal—Sasha" Clove stuttered, breaking the silence and nearly forgetting the pretense. The faun pointed into the distance down the ruined road. "Is that them?"

Galessel looked where Clove pointed, knowing she'd asked because her eyesight was better. There were indeed three figures making their way back over the uneven ground. A knot in her chest loosened. "Yes, I think so, though your eyes are better than mine, boss."

N'hena's wings started beating, speeding up until they blurred, and she lifted several feet off the deck. "If you'll excuse me, I need to see to collecting our friends." She flew toward the bow of the ship, her orders a little less barky than normal.

Galessel was somewhat glad to see N'hena go. Keeping up the pretense of being Sasha was hard, and she'd had to keep herself from addressing N'hena as she normally would—with much more familiarity than an unknown human would ever think to have. Now that they were away from the palace, she wondered at letting everyone in on the ruse. But there was still a price on her head, and though she could trust those on this ship, it would be harder for everyone to keep the secret if they knew. Someone would slip. She just hoped it wasn't her.

Navarre called out once he was within shouting distance, and N'hena maneuvered the ship low enough for them to lower a water barrel over the side.

"Forgive me, my friends, but you'll have to leave your clothes. I can see from here that you're covered in dust, and we can't have you bringing cold-iron on board. Wash yourselves, then we'll hoist you up."

Morgan glanced down at her leather coat and swore before taking it off and throwing it to the side. "Damn. I really liked that coat."

Navarre looked awful. What had he seen in the city that pulled at him so? His clothes and hair were dusty grey and his face was haggard. The two women looked no better. There were clean areas around their eyes, where Navarre's face was uniformly grey. Galessel recognized the sign of tears hastily wiped away.

As the humans stripped and washed, N'hena's crew set up a hoist system and sent down a crate for their cleaned weapons. The captain wasn't taking any chances. Everyone was pulled up individually, after having one of the others wash off their feet. Samga was the last to come up, having washed her own feet in an interesting balancing act on the chair-like hoist, ending with tossing the contaminated rag to the ground.

Galessel stayed one step behind Clove as they went to meet their human cohorts, but it was hard. She wanted nothing more than to run to Navarre and hold him.

"What news?" Clove asked as crew members brought Navarre, Morgan, and Samga fresh clothes. The humans seemed unperturbed by their nakedness.

The Intrepid lurched as her engines spun up to speed and they took to the air. Galessel didn't blame N'hena for wanting to put a great deal of distance between them and this poisoned land.

"It's as the queen mother suspected. The fionnagh is gone. Those bastards destroyed it, and everything around it, with cold-iron grenades." Morgan said. Her face was deep red and her hands were held in white-knuckled fists.

Navarre looked briefly at Galessel, his eyes full of unshed tears, before switching his gaze to Clove and addressing her. It hurt her a little to be skipped over, but she reminded herself Navarre was better at this undercover thing than she was.

"Now that our suspicions are proven, I have no doubt the Hammer Guardians' plan is to destroy them all, or at least enough of them to cripple the Hidden Lands and make the remainder easier to conquer," he said.

Clove's fur rippled, and her ears turned back in anger. "We have to stop them. There are only four left according to her majesty, Vallanon, the home of the Oak-kin; Dunngrimm, the capital of the D'zur; the Unseelie capital of SoulScar; and Soji's island of Vasyann." Clove pulled a map from one of the pouches at her waist and handed it to Navarre. "We know Soji's a target, but she's at the other end of the realm. What do you think their next target will be?"

Galessel, having traveled to all but SoulScar, knew where each was in relation to Alexandria. While Navarre studied the map, she tried the ferret out the next target as well. The Oak-kin were closest, being just across the Strait of Harzon to the south. The fionnagh of the D'zur was likely deep within one of their underground cities and would be a difficult target for the humans to get to. SoulScar was an unknown. She had no idea if the Unseelie would ally with the Hammer Guardians and Svellvega or not. They were an unpredictable lot. She was about to whisper in Clove's ear when Navarre spoke.

"If this map is accurate at all, the next target has to be Vallanon. It's the closest. As for the next after that, I don't know, but if we're to succeed in defending them, we need to get ahead of the Hammer Guardians. We need to get word to each location as soon as possible, which means we'll need to split up." He looked to Clove. "Am I right in assuming there's a Moon Gate near each of these locations?"

Clove nodded. "We can go back to the Gate at Saya and break off from there."

"Good," Navarre said. "I don't know these places and peoples well enough to determine who would be best where. Clove, do you and Sasha have suggestions?"

Galessel whispered with Clove for a moment before she took a step back, placing herself again behind the faun.

"Eirsal should take ten of the Anisbarii and go to SoulScar. The Unseelie might be more likely to let him past the border than any of the humans. Samga, take ten as well and go to Vallanon. You're in touch with nature enough to be able to relate to the Oak-kin. Morgan, take another contingent of Anisbarii to Dunngrimm. They greet each other with insults. Act as if you're starting a bar fight, and you'll do fine. Navarre, you and Sasha should go to Vasyann. She's studied Soji and will know how to talk to them."

"And what about you, Clove? Will you come with Sasha and I?" Navarre asked.

The faun shook her head and laid her ears back. "I'm going to see if N'hena wants to go hunting the airship they're using. I want to shoot them out of the sky before they get to the next target."

Everyone nodded and, with grim faces, parted to prepare for their individual missions. Navarre said he would find Eirsal, who was below decks recovering, and let him know the plan. Galessel hugged Clove when no one was watching and returned to their room to pack while Clove went to find N'hena and enjoin her to a hunt of the Svellvega airship. It wouldn't take much, if any convincing. The sylph captain had long been looking to avenge the attack that had damaged both Galessel and *The Intrepid*.

Galessel wondered at her own lack of tears, or anger, or anything as she went through her supplies and double checked she had her House sigils to show Soji. It wasn't like her to be numb, especially in the face of so much death and destruction. It was a strange feeling, and she didn't like it. She made a mental note to ask Navarre if he experienced such a lack of feelings while at war. Of anyone she knew, he'd know how to deal with it.

She prayed to the Goddess they'd be able to save the remaining fionnagh. Only time would tell if her prayers would be answered.

Chapter 8
Vallanon

amga ran her hand down the arm of her elven silk coat. She liked the feel of the green fabric. It was soft but durable, and like the silk of home, it worked well at regulating temperature. It had kept her warm on the deck of the airship and cool here in the muggy, sun-filled meadows of the forests of Vallanon, the home of the Oak-kin.

She and her cohort of elves stalked through the giant trees, blending into the shadows cast by trunks reaching three hundred feet or more into the air. The elves were as silent as any Shenzhou hunter, causing Samga to wonder if it was magic that quieted the lacquered armor or some method of manufacture. She wore some of it herself, a loan, along with the silken coat, loose pants, and tunic beneath it. The armor appeared to change color, or absorb it, making the elven soldiers nearly impossible to see if you didn't know what to look for. She still mourned the loss of her quilted silk coat, though it had been necessary to leave it behind to prevent making the fae sick. Her mother had made the coat for her, and Samga could imagine being scolded for its loss as her mother prepared roasted rabbit and steamed rice in the family yurt.

One of the soldiers, a scout named Ellisar, stepped out of a shadow before her.

"Hold, honored archer. I hear trouble ahead but hesitate to push forward. Will you scout, and let us know if there is a threat of cold-iron?" The elf looked young, even by elven standards, and his anxiety showed. Samga could tell they were all afraid. As well they should be. She'd seen the damage cold-iron did to Eirsal—the infused steam ball had melted his wing. A bullet made of cold-iron would have killed him.

"My ears do not hear what yours do. Point me in the right direction, and I will scout ahead," Samga said.

"Tell the others to wait near the last clearing we passed. If you hear the scream of an eagle, it is safe to join me. The roar of a bear means come to me, but be cautious and ready to fight. If it is not safe at all, I will report back to you at the clearing."

The elf told her of what he'd heard and where and then disappeared back into the shadows of the forest.

Samga made her way to the next clearing, her eyes darting from one massive tree trunk to the next, each as wide as a townhouse in Arturia. If she hadn't seen these trees for herself, she never would have believed they existed. Whole families could live comfortably in a house nestled in the branches. She imagined some race of fae probably did.

Peeking around the bole of a younger tree, she sucked in a breath. Before her were several tree-like creatures nearly twenty feet tall with skin that looked like bark. They were cowering together before five men all dressed in similar black suits who were pointing guns at them. Hammer Guardians. Two of the Oak-kin were turning a sickly yellow and both oozed what looked like sap from wounds in their torsos.

In the center of the clearing was the fionnagh. With a stouter, larger base that appeared to grow out of the earth, it looked more tree-like than the drawing of the one in the centaur's land. Interwoven branches at the top of the thirty-foot pillar cradled a teardrop-shaped crystal. This one did not look like stone. It looked alive. Not quite a tree, but not solely something worked either.

Samga pulled back the string on her bow, taking aim at a man kneeling before an open lead box. She roared like a bear from the caves near her village and fired. The arrow found its mark through the kneeling man's eye and out the back of his skull. Almost as one, the men turned around, their guns pointing in all directions. She let loose another arrow, felling another almost before the first hit the ground. The lid on the lead box fell closed with an audible thunk. The men started firing randomly, forcing Samga to take cover behind a tree.

Seeing the elves approach, she signaled them to take cover and then waited for the pause in gunfire that meant the Hammer Guardians were reloading. When she heard it, she signaled the elves forward. The elves were faster and reached the clearing before she could even find a target. She watched in horror as one of the men fired off several rounds, wounding two elves in the process. They hadn't all been reloading. She should have known better.

Samga took aim at the active gunman and fired. Her arrow found its mark at the same time the man was picked up and ripped apart like a wishbone by a pair of Oak-kin. The creatures moved at incredible speed, and Samga stood in awe as another of the Hammer Guardians was pulled into the ground by what looked like thick roots snaking out from the foot of another of the tree creatures. Screaming, the man dropped his gun, scrabbling at the earth. His cries were silenced by the earth folding over him as he was pulled completely under.

Looking for another target, Samga turned in time to see one of the elves behead the last Hammer Guardian with a pair of short swords. With a disgusted look on his face, the elf wiped his blades clean on the jacket of the corpse. Samga lowered her bow and surveyed the scene.

The two creatures who'd been shot were gone. All that was left of them were two yellow piles of ash. The grass around them was wilted and yellow. Near the edge of the clearing, the other Oak-kin talked to one another, their speech sounding like rustling branches and occasional low-toned vibrations.

Screams of pain drew Samga's attention behind her. The two elves who had been shot were quickly succumbing to the poison of the cold-iron. They writhed in pain on the forest floor, their faces contorting, turning green. Before anyone could reach them, both dissolved into green goo. Samga stood in shock for what felt like an eternity.

Dropping to her knees, she prayed their suffering had been brief. Young Ellisar had been one of the ones who'd been killed. She'd hoped Eirsal's wound was the worst cold-iron injury she'd see, but this would haunt her.

The remaining elves gathered around the spot where their fellows had died and began to sing.

What shant be lost in all the din will be your names upon the wind.

Names flow like wine upon our lips, while you sail away on ancient ships.

While you sail away from the Hidden Lands, hearts hold you close with a thousand strands.

And though the strands fall broken now, we will fight on if the fates allow.

The rustle of leaves and a touch on her shoulder brought Samga around to face one of the Oak-kin. She craned her neck to look up at the creature's craggy, sorrowful face.

"We have known few humans," the Oak-kin began, its voice low and rustly. "And lately none that are good, but you are one of the honorable ones. You have our gratitude for your aid this day."

"I only wish we would have arrived sooner. You have my deepest regrets for the loss of your kin. I must ask, do you know if there are more of the men like the ones that were here, in your forest?"

The creak of wood accompanied a shake of the Oak-kin's head. "There are six humans in all of Vallanon. Five of them will nevermore hear the wind in our leaves, and the sixth stands before us as a lifelong friend to the forest peoples."

Another of the tree people approached and bowed, its body sounding like the subtle flex of a bow. "We would like to remove the remains from our forest, but the evil they use as weapons is still upon the bodies. May we impose upon you to remove it for us?"

Samga looked around the clearing. Most of the Hammer Guardians had extra ammunition belts, as well as the weapons and the lead case. They were lucky so few had died today. She nodded to the Oak-kin and then conferred with the elves for a moment before setting to the task of collecting all of the cold-iron she could. She knew she'd need to retrieve the bullets from the remains of the elves, but she would let their fellows mourn a little longer before she set to that grisly task. She blinked back tears at the thought of Ellisar's life cut short.

At each corpse her anger intensified. Not only were they all carrying extra cold-iron ammunition, many also had a dagger or two made of the vile stuff. What had the fae ever done to these people to make them so hateful? She didn't understand genocide in her own world, much less the desire to destroy such a beautiful place as the Hidden Lands. Was it so hard to let others be?

The elves and Oak-kin helped her find all of the stray bullets, and with tears in her eyes, Samga deposited the last of the cold-iron into the lead box. She felt horrible for having to further defile the Oak-kin and elven remains, but the cold-iron that killed them was already having an effect on the ground around them. A spare bow string served to lash closed the latch on the box.

The Oak-kin, with nothing more to hinder them, began to hum. The earth around the bodies of the humans, the remains of their kin, and the elves began to vibrate, and the bodies sank silently into the earth. The forest went silent for a moment, even the birds observing a final goodbye. Without another word, the Oak-kin melted back into the forest, and the birds began to sing again.

Shouldering one of the more powerful guns, Samga picked up the lead box with the aid of one of her compatriots, and they began the hike back to the Moon Gate.

Looking back over her shoulder before stepping through the Moon Gate, Samga took in the view of the impossibly giant forest. A child of the steppe herself, the trees were somewhat imposing, but she knew Morgan would love it here; the many shades of green mirrored Morgan's home on the island of Eire.

With a sigh and a silent goodbye, she stepped through the Gate.

Chapter 9
Chaos II

Eirsal stepped through the Moon Gate, his stomach fluttering much like his wings used to. He could flex and move his new wooden and brass prosthetic wings, but they didn't sway in the breeze like his own had. He still ached for the organic feel of the wind. The professor was skilled, but he hadn't mastered sensations yet.

Damned cold-iron. He wished he could stuff the Hammer Guardians full of it and watch them dissolve, but they were immune. Vowing to find something that would kill them slowly, he stepped out of the way of the gate and into the dim meadow. Grey, twisted trees closed in around the gate, and green mist crept along the ground, its reaching tentacles pulling back when they touched the sunlight.

The diminutive sylph was soon surrounded by his much taller elven companions, who all looked as nervous as he felt. They were deep in the heart of the Unseelie kingdom. While there hadn't been open war between the Unseelie and the Anisbarii realms in millennia, the fae of the Unseelie were less than friendly on an auspicious day and downright murderous on a bad one. To make matters worse, this Moon Gate had deposited them in Chaosii, the home of the redcaps.

"Be vigilant," Maiele, the captain of their troop, stated. "Instructor Ivaran wasn't exaggerating in history lessons when he said redcaps are the most murderous beings outside of a pissed off brownie troop. And unlike brownies, redcaps live for blood. Let's not give them ours."

Several elves shuddered at the thought. Eirsal flexed his back muscles, feeling the weight of his new wings and the pack underneath his blue fairy-silk coat.

"Thanks for that, Maiele," Eirsal said. "Maybe that will spur us to walk faster to SoulScar. We'll get there in eight days instead of ten."

The elf maid curled a lip at Eirsal. "You first, fearless leader."

Eirsal looked up at her, catching her smile as he took up the lead. He'd known the red-headed elf for a long time, and they'd always bantered like siblings.

A wailing wind blew through the trees and tried to topple Eirsal. In its wake appeared nearly twenty redcaps riding translucent red horses. The horses moved so quickly, the elves didn't have a chance to move before they were surrounded.

Eirsal had never seen a redcap in person. The beings were about his size—about knee height to an elf—but that's where the similarities ended. Wingless, they had unruly heads of rust-colored hair and double rows of pointed teeth in overly wide mouths. He guessed their hair was actually white, but because redcaps stored their victims' blood in their caps, which were at the moment laid over the necks of their mounts, it was likely some of that blood dripped into their hair, staining it.

Eirsal tried not to look at their caps. It was hard to see through the moving mist of their mounts' manes, but he was pretty sure the caps were dripping wet with blood. He slowly moved his hand to the grip of his hydronium pistol.

"Now there, little sylph, hand off the gun. You've come through our Moon Gate, but you haven't paid the blood toll," one of the redcaps said. His teeth were more jagged than the others, and he held himself straighter. The other redcaps laughed.

The redcap laughter sounded like a metal key dragging across glass. It was all Eirsal could do not to cover his ears. He eased his hand away from his gun, but the elves did not lower their weapons. He smiled at the leader and said, "A toll? Is that what redcaps call hospitality? Are we not guests in your fine realm, or would you dispense with the Laws of Hospitality? I, Eirsal Firewing, emissary of the sylph peoples of Seiya, demand the Rights of Hospitality as befits a servant of the Anisbarii kingdom for myself and my retinue of royal elven guards." He took a breath and continued, "We do not come to your realm empty-handed. We, in fact, bring you an offer of great sport—one that is worthy of the redcap people."

The leader scoffed. "I, Adishro of the Royal Redcap Hunt, do recognize you, Eirsal Firewing, and all your retinue as guests of the Chaosii peoples for the next twenty-four hours. As to your offer, it remains to be seen if it is worthy."

Eirsal placed one hand over his chest and bowed. "Very well. There are humans here in the Hidden Lands, from a group called the Hammer Guardians—" The redcaps all snarled at the name. "—and they are headed to SoulScar to destroy your fionnagh, and through that, the entire Unseelie Court. If you take us there, you will get to feast on their blood, and it will make you strong."

Adishro stroked his chin for a moment. "Hmmm. That does sound like worthy sport for us, but why would we need to take you with us? I'm afraid for you, that you will just have to pay the toll with your lives." The other redcaps on their steeds moved closer and some licked their lips. The elves stood their ground.

Eirsal smiled. He thought that might be their answer, but he knew they loved to wager almost as much as they loved to murder. "Well then, how about a little wager? If I win, you and a band of your people have to get us to SoulScar before nightfall and protect us with your lives. If I lose, you get to kill me and soak up my blood with your cap. All I ask is whatever you do, please don't make me race you." He did his best to look pitiful and waved his prosthetic wings.

The redcap leader grinned, his pointed teeth glinting.

He eyed Eirsal's wings. "I accept your offer of a wager in accordance with the Laws of Hospitality. However, as host, it is I who get to choose what the wager will be, and I choose...that we race!"

The redcap host cheered, and their steeds snorted breaths of red mist.

Eirsal could feel the elves' eyes on him, and he prayed they'd hold just a little longer. They knew this might happen. He looked at the ground and scuffed a line in the dirt with his toe. "Very well. But as a guest, may I place one stipulation?"

Adishro nodded, still grinning.

"That as this is a wager between you and I, you cannot have aid from any living being—and that includes your zephyr steed. I shall abide by the same conditions. It is my hope your people are not as swift of foot as legends claim."

"I accept your conditions." Adishro jumped from the back of his zephyr. It was a good six foot drop but the redcap landed light as a feather. "As host, I state that whosoever reaches the yellow malveli tree first shall be decreed the winner by all assembled here. And, as I am a gracious host, I grant you a head start. For you see, we are quite swift of foot, you foolish sylph. You may have stood a chance were your injuries not quite so severe. But please, let us not tarry. My cap is thirsty for your blood." The redcap waved his bloody cap toward the yellow malveli tree.

Eirsal judged the gnarled, mustard-yellow tree to be about a hundred yards away. He glanced at the elves, who all looked at him with a mixture of dread and hope. He shook hands with the redcap, and then sprinted for the tree, giving it everything he could. He flapped his wings, hoping to gain more speed, but they did little to aid him. He was barely running faster than an elven toddler who'd stolen an ice fruit. He looked back over his shoulder. All of the elves were hanging their heads in shame or resignation.

He'd gotten maybe fifty feet away when he heard Adishro yell, "Ready or not, your blood is mine!"

Within a few seconds the redcap sped past him. Eirsal smiled, and yanked on the cord hanging from the front of his vest. His wings snapped into a rigid flight position and the jetpack under his jacket roared to life. Shouting in relief—the jetpack didn't always ignite immediately—he kicked himself off the ground, letting the jet propel him into the air.

Adishro looked up in time to see Eirsal fly past him.

The sylph gave the redcap credit. Adishro managed to find even more speed, but by the time he got to the tree, Eirsal was already touching it with a single finger as he hovered above the ground.

Shouts of elation from the elves clashed with screams of rage from the redcaps as Eirsal and Adishro returned to the gathering.

"Not fair, sylph. You cheated, which violates the Laws of Hospitality. I will kill you and your entire troupe where you stand." Adishro growled. His chest was heaving and his face was red, with exertion or rage or both, Eirsal couldn't tell.

Eirsal held up his hands to forestall the slaughter. "Not so fast, my friend. In what way did I break the wager? I stated, and you agreed, that neither of us could receive aid from any living being. Neither my wooden wings nor my jetpack are living beings. They are mechanical marvels, to be sure, created by the famed gnome, Professor Fizzlespring. But even he could not render them alive."

Much to Eirsal's relief, Adishro burst into laughter, soon followed by his fellows. Some laughed so hard they fell off their steeds.

The elves did not relax or even crack a smile.

"You are clever, my little friend. Clever indeed. It seems we will not be dining on your blood this day. At least not for another twenty-three hours at any rate." The redcaps laughed again, but this time there was an edge of malice to it. "We will take you to SoulScar, though you may not survive the trip if you wish to be there in a day." Adishro motioned Eirsal and the elves to approach one of the zephyrs. "As you may have guessed, these are not ordinary zephyrs." He smiled widely, showing off his teeth. "These are, of course, blood zephyrs. They will take you anywhere you want to go, as long as you give them blood."

Several of the elves backed away, but Maiele did not. Instead she asked the question no one else wanted to ask. "And how do you propose we do that?"

"A simple cut to the hand will do it. Lay your cut palm on their neck. As long as you touch them, your wound will not close and will not stop bleeding," Adishro explained.

"How quickly can these beasts get us to SoulScar? The Hammer Guardians will likely arrive there by airship, and they have a head start on us." Maiele was all business.

Adishro made a point to eye each elf. "With enough urging, the blood zephyrs can get us there in two hours, maybe a little more if you're stingy with your blood."

"And will we arrive there alive?"

Adishro shrugged. "I promised to get you there alive, didn't I?"

Eirsal could tell Maiele wasn't happy with that answer, and to be honest, he wasn't either. But they didn't have much of a choice.

They mounted the restless zephyrs and cut their palms. Eirsal's mount shivered at the touch of blood on its neck. It took all of Eirsal's willpower not to pull his hand away when the sucking sensation started. If the fate of the Hidden Lands wasn't at stake, he would have jumped off the beast and headed straight back to Anisbar.

He looked to his elven compatriots. All of them looked a little white in the knuckles, but they all held their palms fast to their mounts. They were committed. Adishro whistled and the zephyrs started running.

Eirsal held on for all he was worth. Trees streamed by impossibly fast. He made the mistake of looking down only once. The ground was passing by so quickly he became dizzy and almost lost his seat. Adishro, riding next to him, smiled widely at Eirsal's discomfort.

After maybe half an hour, Eirsal's equilibrium adjusted to the speed of zephyrs, and he was able to take a more relaxed seat on his mount. He started to look around at the forest they were traversing. They were going too fast to see many details, but he could tell the forest wasn't as dense as some, and the zephyrs seemed to be following an established road. The trees were thin and grew out of a tangled underbrush.

Without warning, something burst out from the side of the road just as Eirsal's mount sped past. Several redcaps yelled behind him, but he couldn't distinguish words over the wind racing past his ears. He looked over his shoulder to a sight he wasn't sure was real. An *agar roch*—a blood unicorn—was chasing them.

Larger than an Arturian draft horse, the beast's hide was the color of old blood. Two curved, pointed horns protruded from its brow, and razor-sharp fangs protruded down from the upper jaw. It snapped at the haunches of the zephyr behind him, barely missing. Fear made Eirsal grip his mount tighter. He wanted nothing more than to urge his steed to faster speed, but they'd never outrun the *agar roch.*

Eirsal drew his pistol and took aim as the blood unicorn pushed forward to take another bite at the redcap. Eirsal fired. The shot hit its mark in the chest of the fearsome beast. The *agar roch* reared back in pain and broke off its pursuit. As the zephyrs rounded a bend in the road, Eirsal saw the creature fall to its knees.

Adishro saluted Eirsal and spurred his zephyr on. The others picked up their pace to keep up with their leader. The suction on Eirsal's palm increased with his zephyr's speed, and he began to feel lightheaded.

The forest around them started to thin, transitioning into a rocky plain. Scraggly bushes and flowering mounds surrounded by curved thorns dotted the landscape. Adishro called a halt and jumped off his zephyr. Eirsal gratefully removed his hand from his steed and cradled it to his chest. It ached to the bone.

He twisted in his seat to see where Adishro had gone and was just in time to see one of the elven guard slump over the neck of his zephyr. The redcap leader held the animal and put a hand to the elf's throat, then removed the hand that seemed stuck to the zephyr's neck and examined it.

"He's still alive, but cut his hand too deeply. These beasts are greedy and will bleed you dry if you let them." Adishro signaled to another redcap. "Crezis, ride behind this one and see that he makes it to SoulScar alive."

The one called Crezis scowled but did as he was bid, climbing up behind the unconscious elf. He pulled a strip of cloth from a belt pouch and handed it to Adishro, who used it to bind the elf's hand.

"Anyone else feeling like they won't make it another hour?" Adishro asked.

Eirsal couldn't tell if the redcap was actually concerned or just hoping for some unintended victims. He suppressed a shudder.

Seeing no one indicate their distress, Adishro mounted his zephyr and waved the group forward.

Taking a deep breath and steeling himself for the vertigo he knew would follow, Eirsal put his cut hand back upon the zephyr's neck and held on as tightly as he could.

CHAPTER 10
SoulScar

SoulScar, the Unseelie capital city, wasn't so much of a city as a fortress carved out of a mountain.

Even at the speed the zephyrs traveled, Eirsal had been able to see it for the last hour. At first merely a misty mountain in the distance across the desert plain, it became an ever larger presence as the terrain changed to a dangerous mix of marshes and quicksand.

Despite lightheadedness from blood loss and the inherent peril of trusting their lives to the redcaps, Eirsal was glad they'd run into them and their zephyr steeds. He was not sure he and his elf companions would have survived the road through the Chaosii forest, much less safely traversed the marshes outside of SoulScar.

He sent up a silent prayer to Chaun for luck. They'd need it if they were to live through the next few hours.

As they drew near SoulScar's frost-rimmed gates—massive things of melted stone and metal, with tortured faces imbedded within—one of the elves shouted, "There! To the west. There's an airship!"

Eirsal halted his steed and shifted to look west, shading his eyes against the sun. He could make out only a black dot in the sky. "What do you see, Cohnal?" he asked.

"Black ship and black sails, Eirsal," the guard replied. "Moving fast. We might have half an hour, maybe a little more, before it gets here."

They had arrived just in time—assuming he could convince the Unseelie Court of the danger before it arrived on their doorstep. Eirsal had hoped for time to rest before presenting himself to the court. The effort it took to keep his eyes open was mounting, but there was no time. "Adishro, can you get us in to see the Court immediately?"

The redcap's feral grin sent chills down Eirsal's back. "Of course, they're right here."

Eirsal turned his steed back around to find the gates opened and a retinue of fae before them. At the head was a beautiful but unlikely pair. Astride an *agar roch*, Damháin, king of the Unseelie had the coloring of an autumn leaf and dreadlocked hair, much like Navarre's. His white eyes were as piercing and cold as icicles. Beside him, sitting sidesaddle on a hippokampus magically supported by a constantly churning wave of water, was his queen, Lorelei. Shrouded in a dress of sea foam, seaweed-green hair framed her pearlescent white face. She smiled, showing a row of serrated teeth.

Behind them were arrayed a variety of fae: creatures of winter, decay, and darkness. To either side of the retinue stood a guard of shadow elementals. Beings of air and darkness, their eyes were pits of the deepest black. Each held a black-handled, toothed-bladed scythe in one ghostly hand.

Eirsal and the elves dismounted, to their detriment. From the corner of his eye, Eirsal saw two of the elven guard fall to their knees, faces pale from blood loss. Cohnal and Maiele, while colorless, kept their hands on their steeds' saddles for support, and the elf who'd passed out earlier simply bowed from his seat on the zephyr—unable or unwilling to dismount. Eirsal used his wings for balance as chills ran in crosscurrents around his body and the world threatened to spin out of control.

"I should kill you now, intruders, for daring to enter our realm without leave," Damháin said in a booming bass voice. He pointed to the growing black speck in the sky. "And what do you bring with you? Word comes to us of humans in the Hidden Lands and the destruction of Alexandria. And now our faithful redcaps arrive on our doorstep with you as their prisoners?"

He turned his attention to Adishro and the redcaps. "Many thanks to you and your kin for bringing these interlopers to us. Sadly, they will die without much of a fight, being weakened as they are by your zephyrs. 'Tis a shame. I was looking forward to some sport."

Adishro, his red cap clutched to his chest, bowed before the Unseelie royals. "No, your majesty, I mean, yes, they will die quickly should you so wish it, but they have made a bargain with us through a fairly won wager. They are protected under the Laws of Hospitality. Not only that, but Eirsal here," Adishro waved his cap toward Eirsal, "saved the life of one of my tribe, and so is owed a life boon. That's been partially repaid through his elf friend here, but they are under our protection, my king, for another nineteen hours."

Damháin scowled, and Lorelei's feral smile faded. Dark clouds began to gather around the peak of the mountain fortress as if in answer to the royals' disappointment.

Eirsal could feel the dark energy rising and rushed forward, fighting vertigo to stay upright. "We beg your forgiveness, your highnesses, for intruding upon your court. I come at the behest of the king and queen of Anisbar to warn you of the human invasion and the threat they pose to you and yours."

Lorelei laughed. "Do the Anisbarii think us so weak as to need warning against a ship of humans? Is it not insult enough their *sikevra* daughter played one of our princes for a fool? Now they send you, a slight, little sylph with toy wings to do—what, exactly?"

Fluttering his wooden wings, he rose to look Lorelei in the eye. It was a calculated risk, but the Unseelie valued strength and defiance. "These humans destroyed the fionnagh in Alexandria. The centaurs and the nightsteeds are gone. No more will they gallop across the Hidden Lands."

Eirsal pointed to the approaching ship, trying to keep his meager altitude with weakening wings. "These humans are coming to destroy your fionnagh. With cold-iron."

The assembly gasped. The world began to close in on him, his vision narrowing to a tunnel, and Eirsal dropped to the ground, unable to regain his feet. Maiele rushed to his side and helped him stand.

Lorelei dismounted from her hippokampus, the magical wave propelling her forward until she stood before Eirsal. She lifted his chin with a cold finger, her teal eyes searching his. "No being of sound mind would risk riding with a tribe of redcaps to deliver a tale of falsehoods. And indeed, more of your kin, Adishro," she said, looking to the redcap, "have told us the tale of the nightsteeds."

She smiled her shark-toothed smile again, and Eirsal felt nauseous.

"What do you think, husband? Should we keep these waifs alive a little longer and have some fun with the humans? I haven't lured one to its death in ages."

"Very well, my love. If they are truly coming with cold-iron, then let us be rid of them." Damháin began chanting in a tongue unknown to Eirsal. The dark clouds crowding the mountain doubled in size and started to sink, coating the fortress in an impenetrable fog.

Taking Eirsal's hand, Lorelei led him and the others into the fortress. Eirsal was not sure what he expected to see once they passed the gates, but a deserted city wasn't it.

The mountain, it appeared, was just a shell, a ring of rock providing a natural defense to the beings within. Obsidian towers filled the central bowl while smaller, crystalline buildings of deep purples, blues, and reds seemed to grow from the ground around them. The fionnagh was likely set deeper into the citadel. Paths of hexagonal basalt wove between buildings and met to form larger thoroughfares.

But there were no residents, no merchants, not even a cat sith or raven lurking in the shadows.

Maiele whispered, "Where is everyone?"

Lorelei grinned. "The power of Damháin is great. All within the walls have been sent to the space between worlds."

There was a collective gasp from the elves at this news. "Why would you do that to your own people?" Maiele asked. Her face, which had been pale from blood loss, gained some color with her anger.

Lorelei cracked a chilling smile. "Oh child, it is of no consequence to the Unseelie. We walk with one foot in the Shadow and can transverse it with ease." Her smile disappeared as she stared at Maiele. "Unlike our fae and Seelie cousins."

Lorelei shrugged and her smile returned. "It is a safe place for our people. Only those here and a few others remain to help in the fight. Even with cold-iron, how hard can humans be to kill?" She giggled with girlish delight.

The redcaps helped the elves and Eirsal behind a low rock outcropping that had been transformed into a stable near the entrance. Directed to sit and recover behind the protection of the mountain rock, they watched with dread as the black airship descended through the clouds and finally stopped, hovering no more than the height of a single-story building above the ground.

There'd been no discussion of a plan. Eirsal pulled a second hydronium gun from his satchel. Larger than his pistol, it had a yellow crystal the size of a troll's thumb in the middle of the barrel. He'd never fired it, but Professor Fizzlespring assured him it would do great damage, even though it had no visible projectiles.

Keeping an eye on the five humans being lowered to the ground by ropes, he filled a reservoir with alcohol that would activate the hydronium in the combustion chamber when he pulled the trigger.

The humans had barely reached the ground when the airship powered up its engines and began to rise.

Eirsal didn't think his gun could do much damage to the airship, so he took aim at the humans instead and waited, letting the elves fire at the ship with their hydronium rifles. A few hit, biting chunks of wood from the hull, but were ultimately ineffective.

As the airship disappeared back into the clouds, Lorelei began to sing. She was sitting in a fountain several yards from where the humans had set down. They all turned toward her, some with guns aimed, but they soon lowered their weapons, and the two carrying a large lead box dropped it. They were completely enthralled by her voice.

Eirsal stepped onto a bucket, rested his arm on the outer rim of the stable, and took aim at the closest human. He fired.

A loud bang preceded the appearance of a yellow beam of light streaking from the barrel of the gun. The beam decapitated the man. The force of the shot knocked Eirsal back several feet, into the far wall of the stable.

Dazed, he stared at the gun until he noticed Maiele looking at him with awe. He held the gun up proudly and said, "Never fired it before, but gods be praised, that Fizzlespring is a genius." Maiele nodded and held out a hand to help him up.

Making his way back to the outer stable wall, Eirsal was just in time to watch the redcaps do what they did best: kill.

They descended upon the humans with ruthless abandon. Adishro jumped on the back of one man, plunging his hand completely through the human's chest and out the other side, the man's still-beating heart in his fist. With a shout, Adishro pulled the heart back through and jumped off the body before it hit the ground.

Presenting the heart to Eirsal and the elves at the wall, he devoured it in ripping bites. Eirsal felt his bile rise. But the carnage didn't stop there. One human went down under a pile of three redcaps as they became a frightening red cloud of teeth and claws around the poor soul. When the redcaps scattered in search of their next victim, there was nothing left but bloody, shredded clothing. Another redcap ripped a third human's throat out, moving so quickly all Eirsal saw was a spray of blood as the man fell to the ground, clutching his throat.

Through all of this, Lorelei kept singing.

The last Hammer Guardian stopped and looked around, his eyes narrowed in a glare, as if annoyed the sounds of the dying were interfering with the music. With a roar, Damháin appeared out of nowhere and crushed the man's skull with an enormous club. Looking around him for another opponent, his shoulders slumped when none presented themselves.

"That is it? That was the invasion force?" Thunder rumbled, and the clouds grew darker. Damháin stalked toward Eirsal and his elven cohorts. "You intruded upon my realm for that?" He raised his club, still dripping blood, above Eirsal's head.

Eirsal couldn't help himself. He cowered, unable to say anything.

Lorelei appeared at Damháin's elbow and put her hand on his arm. "Now husband, let's not be rash." She smiled at Maiele. "While they're weak, and we could easily pawn off their deaths as the fault of the humans, I think we should keep them. They're all so pretty, even the sylph with his fantastical wooden wings. We can keep them as thralls. I could use some new playthings. The winters here get so lonely."

Eirsal was fairly sure she batted her eyelashes at Damháin. The Unseelie King lowered his club, and Eirsal finally took a breath.

"Your majesty, if I may," Eirsal said. "As you saw, the humans themselves were not the threat. It's what they carried with them in the box that is the true threat. If you open it, I believe you'll find it is full of cold-iron. That is what they were going to use to destroy your fionnagh."

At the mention again of cold-iron, the Unseelie host drew back. Damháin's face darkened and Lorelei hissed.

Pushing on, Eirsal said, "You could make us slaves or kill us, but that would still leave the cold-iron in your midst." He gestured to the lead box. "Or, you could let us live, and we'll promise to take the cold-iron far from your lands and never return."

Damháin looked down on Eirsal. "You bested the redcaps, clever sylph, but I'm Damháin, king of the Unseelie. You will not trick me so easily. I will call your bluff. There is no cold-iron in that box."

Eirsal could do nothing but tell the truth. "I do not jest, your majesty, and I will bet my life on it. If there is no cold-iron in that box, then you may do with us what you will, for we cannot stop you. But if there is, then I ask that your people lead us, without harm, to the nearest Moon Gate, that we may depart your lands and take the cold-iron with us."

The king of the Unseelie stared down at Eirsal for a long moment, then turned to the elves, lingering the longest on those still recovering. "You all are either very stupid or very brave for coming here today. I will take your bet, little sylph."

"With your leave, I will go open the box, your majesty," Eirsal offered.

Damháin put his massive hand on Eirsal's diminutive shoulder. "No. You could easily feign sickness without anyone being the wiser." He turned to a hag who had appeared nearby. "Bertina, open the box so we may dispense with these charlatans once and for all."

The hag had appeared out of nowhere, apparently at Damháin's silent summoning, but SoulScar remained unpopulated except for those who took part in the brief altercation with the Hammer Guardians. Eirsal inwardly commended Damháin for being cautious.

Bertina appeared to be in her middle years. Like all hags, she had a long nose with a few warts, but not as many as she would have when she reached her full power in another fifty years or so. She walked mostly upright with just a slight hunch in her shoulders as she approached the lead box. Pulling back her hood to expose salt and pepper hair, she unhooked the latch and threw back the lid, stepping back a few paces as she did so. When nothing jumped out or exploded, she stepped back in and bent over the box briefly before reeling back.

Bertina clutched her stomach and croaked, "Cold-iron, my lord. Leather belts full of projectiles and many round things that look like bombs." She staggered back, her skin turning an even more sickly shade of green than normal.

One redcap standing near her pushed her farther out of the way and looked inside himself. He quickly succumbed to the effects of the cold-iron and doubled over in pain. The ground around the box began to crack and flake.

With an angry roar, Damháin leapt for the box, closing the lid with a swipe of his great club. The cries of the affected fae fell to whimpers. He turned back to Eirsal. Blue flames danced above his head. "Fell sylph! What have you done to my people? You will die for this!" He stepped toward Eirsal with his club held high.

Eirsal resisted the urge to shrink back, instead standing his ground. Fickle Unseelie. They were even worse than the Svellvega. Why should he be blamed for this since he was the one who'd warned the king of what lay inside? Just as the club started its downward swing, Lorelei stepped in front of Damháin and kissed him.

The king instantly calmed and lowered his club.

"Surely this was not Eirsal's fault, my love. He did warn you. Let us honor our agreement and allow the sylph and his elven companions to live and leave our lands." Lorelei turned her attention to Eirsal but kept one hand on the king, who gazed at her with adoration. "Please give our thanks to the Anisbarii court for sending such brave emissaries to help save our people. Adishro, you and your folk shall lead these fine fae safely to the nearest Moon Gate so that they may return to Anisbar without delay."

She kissed her husband again and began to lead him away, but stopped after a few steps and looked over her shoulder. "And Eirsal, I would not visit SoulScar again for a long while." She waved him and the elves off. "Now take that evil box of death with you and go."

Lorelei, Damháin, and the hag all faded from view, leaving only the redcaps and Eirsal's group in the deserted courtyard.

Eirsal felt faint at the idea of getting back on the zephyrs. He wasn't sure he or the elves would survive the trip. Thankfully, Adishro seemed to come to the same conclusion. The redcap whistled and six zephyrs appeared, hitched to a black carriage that in Arturia, would have been easily mistaken for a macabre hearse. Enormous bat wings formed the passenger compartment, while thick rose canes, complete with thorns, formed the hitch. Adishro opened the door and beckoned for them to enter.

Maiele looked to Eirsal, the skepticism clear in her eyes. Eirsal shrugged. "Even without the queen's order, we still have eighteen hours, more or less, of good faith under the first bargain. I say we take our chances."

Maiele nodded and made her way over to the lead box. She secured the latch and picked it up, holding it as far from her body as she could. The rest of the company boarded the carriage, and they settled the box firmly under one of the seats.

Adishro closed the carriage door with a wicked smile and disappeared. Eirsal heard him shouting to the zephyrs before the carriage lurched forward and sped from SoulScar.

Chapter 11
Dunngrimm

urik moved the wheel to the left and adjusted the altitude lever, pulling *Death's Embrace* over a snow-capped mountain peak. His breath fogged the inside of the cabin's window. He hated the cold. It reminded him too much of DawnGuard and his father. He couldn't be done with this part of the mission fast enough.

Turbulence, caused by crosswinds over the numerous peaks in the Lunenrial Range, rocked the ship, but Murik flattened out the jostling by flipping a few switches and sending a stern thought through his blood connection to the ship's stabilizers. The blood-bond made the entire ship feel like an extension of his body. It was a thrilling experience to fly this way, and one that no longer took all his concentration.

One peak, larger than the rest in girth, not height, loomed in front of him. The mountaintop was flat, missing the razor-edged angles and cliffs of the others around it. As he approached, its hollow nature became more apparent in the moonlight. Legend said the mountain of the D'zur (a race the humans called dwarves—why they had to make up their own name baffled him) was once a violent volcano, but the only fire within it now was in the forges of the D'zur, deep in its core.

Murik cut back on the engines and eased *Death's Embrace* over the edge of the crater, lowering the ship into the shadows. Sheer grey walls closed in around the ship as it descended. When moonlight no longer illuminated the way, he was tempted to flip the toggle that would turn on the running lamps, but he resisted. Stealth was required for this part of his delivery. He'd made arrangements, but it always paid to be wary.

A thousand feet below the top of the crater's rim, a maze of stone pathways and docks appeared, anchored to the rocks with enormous iron chains. Lights, powered by sunstones, cast the docks in a twilight glow. Docks, consisting of various-sized platforms, spiraled down along the inside of the mountain—one of the many lifelines providing outside goods and trade to the D'zur.

The docks seemed unnaturally quiet. Murik began to feel uneasy. He hoped his contact hadn't betrayed him.

A blue light flashed at the edge of a platform just down and to the right of the ship. Murik adjusted course and settled *Death's Embrace* a few feet from it.

Pulling the ship's communication tube down from its clip above his left shoulder, Murik spoke into the conical vocal funnel. "Ready your men, Kane, but keep them on deck until I give the signal to disembark."

He couldn't be done with the humans fast enough. They smelled. And Kane was always questioning his motives and, at times, his tactics.

Locking the wheel into place and activating the blood-bond wards, Murik toggled the switch to lower the gangplank.

On the platform, a blue fog hugged the stone, rising to Murik's waist as he stepped off the gangplank. Before him stood a dusky-skinned D'zur. Typical of his kind, he wore a short-trimmed beard and tattoos covered his naked torso. The dwarf was bald but for a topknot of long red hair. He held a blue lantern. There were so many platforms inside the cone of the mountain that Murik never would have found the right one without aid. He gave the D'zur credit. Dunngrimm was a near-impenetrable stronghold, and the maze and sheer number of docks typically made this avenue of invasion impossible. Unless you had inside help.

Murik nodded to the D'zur but said nothing, noticing the prone forms of other D'zur scattered about the platform. His unease lightened.

"You got twenty ticks to get in and get out 'afore the dock workers wake up," the D'zur said. He spoke softly and his voice was muffled by the elaborate breathing apparatus he was wearing. Tubes snaked from a tank on his back to a mask that obscured his nose and mouth. Soft clicks and whirs came, presumably, from whatever mechanism powered the device.

Red Top, the name Murik had given his contact for lack of knowledge of his actual name, held out his meaty hand.

Unhooking a large leather coin purse from his belt, Murik placed it in Red Top's hand. The D'zur opened the purse and pulled out a fist-sized pink diamond. He held it up to the light of the blue lamp, and after a moment, he nodded and replaced the diamond. Red Top turned on his heel and disappeared down a nearby tunnel.

His business finished, Murik signaled to the humans waiting on the deck of his ship. They stunk with the scent of impatience. He shook off his revulsion, reminding himself this was almost over. Soon, he would watch the Hidden Lands burn. Or rather, disappear.

Murik waited for the man carrying the lead box to disembark before pushing past the others up the gangplank. As soon as Murik reached the top, he willed the ship to pull away, forcing the last human to jump, earning himself a string of epithets as the man landed on his fellows.

"Blasted fly! If Cap'n Kane doesn't murder the bastard, I'm going to," the last man cursed.

The last bit echoed off the steep walls of the cavern.

Murik laughed as he took the wheel. "We'll just see who the fly is, now won't we, little man?" he said to himself. "Good luck getting through the rest of the tunnels." He pulled a lever, spun the wheel, and guided his ship up toward the light of the moon.

❀ ❀ ❀

The spacious cavern should have been pitch black, carved as it was out of the heart of an extinct volcano.

Instead, it was lit in soft pastels by a rainbow's worth of glowing crystals embedded in the walls. Many had been carved by D'zur artisans into shapes that amplified their ambient light or created intricate shadows on the cavern walls.

Morgan adjusted her seat, trying to find a more comfortable position on the hard leather saddle keeping her on the back of the giant cave bat. Luckily, her mount, like the others around her, was not hanging upside down as bats in Ashelon were wont to do. Ten elves and ten D'zur sat on their own bat mounts to either side of her, perched on the railing of a bridge.

Though heights didn't normally affect her, the sheer scope of the place took her breath away. Doorways were carved into the walls in a haphazard pattern, while bridges connected them across the expanse. Only when she looked down (or up) at the crisscrossed bridges did the lacework spider web pattern appear. Nestled in the center of the web of bridges sat the fionnagh, surrounded by a white crystal gazebo.

From their position above, the roof of the gazebo radiated the pastel hues of the fionnagh within. Morgan had been fortunate enough to see the structure up close earlier. The base of the fionnagh was formed from solid, vivid blue stone which rose to support a sphere of crystals that glowed with every hue of the rainbow.

Normally the D'zur capital would be alive with the sounds of mining, commerce, and life, but the place was now silent. Only the echoing voices of the approaching humans could be heard. Morgan and her elven cohort had been lucky to outrace the Svellvega ship, and the D'zur battle lord, Spinel Opalforged, had been more than willing to evacuate her people to the deeper reaches of the city for safety.

Celsian, a D'zur communication specialist, relayed the position of the humans every few minutes. The system of geocurrent relays was a revelation to Morgan. She'd never heard of its like, and it remained a complete mystery to her even after a lengthy explanation, but for the D'zur it was an incredibly fast and accurate communication system. Celsian held out his headset that encapsulated the vibration amplifiers to Morgan. "They're close."

Morgan fitted the leather-covered amplifiers over her ears. The gruff voices of the invading Hammer

Guardians came through the device with such clarity, she had to check they weren't right next to her.

"Well, I gotta say, these stone munchers know how to build stuff, Silas. That's stunning."

"I wonder how long it took to build all this. There must be thousands of statues in these hallways. There's nothing like this back home," another voice said.

"If you're done sightseeing, we've got work to do, lads. This hallway is the perfect spot for an ambush. Let's go."

The last voice sounded familiar to Morgan, but she couldn't put a name to the voice. She'd had so many run-ins with the anti-fae group that the members blended together into a single bigoted thug in her mind.

She handed the amplifiers back to Celsian and turned her gaze to follow where one of the elves was pointing.

On the far side of the cavern, the invaders were slowly walking out of the tunnel entrance near one of the bridges leading straight to the fionnagh. The lack of handrails on the landing and the bridge seemed to cause them to pause just as much as the epic sight before them.

The bat riders tensed, and their mounts began to extend and stretch their wings in preparation for flight. There was a loud click as the first of the humans stepped out onto the bridge. The men froze for a moment before continuing. When they reached the halfway point to the fionnagh, there was another click. This time, a section of the bridge fell away, tumbling onto the bridges below it with a thundering crash that drowned out the cries of the two men who fell with it.

Together, the bats tipped forward, free-falling off the rail. Morgan gripped the saddle and reins with all her strength as her mount hurtled toward the fionnagh. The wind in her face was warm and tinged with the metallic scent of the forges deep below them. Only after her bat spread its wings and her butt was firmly back in its seat did she draw in a breath. What a rush!

The zing of a bullet passing by her ear brought Morgan's attention back to the task at hand. Trusting the bat to follow the pressure of her knees, she let go of the reins, drew her pistols, and returned fire.

A pain-filled shriek off to her right drew her attention in time to see a bat plummet past her, the poor beast dead beneath its rider, the victim of a cold-iron bullet. Below her, a Hammer Guardian's cheer was cut short as sharp claws gripped him briefly, pulling him off the bridge and dropping him over the abyss. He quit screaming after colliding with the third bridge.

Morgan urged her mount forward, alternating pressure with her knees to guide the bat into a zigzag pattern to avoid the frenzied shots of the remaining men below.

A D'zur rider swooped down, narrowly missing one of the men, who'd managed to duck just in time. It was enough of a diversion that the brute didn't see the second D'zur, who'd leapt from his mount and was now aiming his war hammer.

Morgan looked away as the D'zur smashed the man's head into pulp.

The remaining Hammer Guardian stopped firing and knelt down before the lead box he'd set down on the bridge, his hands in the air. "I surrender!"

Morgan pulled her bat into a hover a few feet from the man. She took the briefest of moments to compensate for the motion caused by bat's flapping wings, and she aimed both of her guns at him. "Drop your weapon."

The Hammer Guardian tossed his gun before him. It clattered on the bridge. He grinned. "If I'm gonna die, I'm taking you dirt munchers with me." He reached forward to open the box.

Morgan fired. Two shots rang out, followed by the hollow clicks of empty chambers. The man reeled from the impact, but was undeterred. He crawled forward, and with a rictus grin, opened the box and pushed it off the bridge before collapsing.

Morgan leapt from her bat. She heard the word "No!" echoing through the cavern and realized it was her voice.

She dove after the box, gasping as the rush of falling pulled the air from her lungs. The box tumbled through the air, staying just out of reach for what seemed like minutes. It was pure luck that the initial tumble had closed the lid. Had it not, cold iron would have rained down, poisoning the lake in the depths of the volcano.

Morgan strained to reach the box until finally, she grasped it, pulling it to her chest.

She saw the bridge, but it was too late.

Morgan rolled to her back just as she collided with the bridge, every muscle tensed to hold the box of cold-iron closed.

Fiery pain ran through her head and chest. Morgan could feel her lifeblood draining away, all of her strength suddenly gone.

Hands propped her up and voices inquired if she was all right, but she couldn't find her voice to reply. As her vision swirled to black, her last thought was of Samga and their last kiss.

❁ ❁ ❁

Samga stepped from the Gate onto the cobblestones of the Anisbar courtyard and collapsed as unbidden tears began to stream down her face. Her chest filled with pain, and she gasped for breath.

The elves rushed to her side. "My lady, what is amiss? Are you injured?"

She could only shake her head as the world shrunk around her. As if from down a long tunnel, she could hear calls for the healers and other aid. Gasping, she waved off the concerned hands of her elven friends. She wasn't hurt, but something was terribly wrong. Why did her heart feel like it was breaking?

Morgan's face appeared before her, a sad smile on her lips. "Carry on without me love. I'll wait for you on the shores of TirNaNog."

No! Samga reached for Morgan's image, but it faded into mist and was gone.

Samga collapsed to the ground, wailing. When she could finally draw breath enough to speak again, all she could say to those who'd crowded around her was, "Morgan's dead."

CHAPTER 12
VALLAZARI

Navarre was unprepared for the warmth and moisture that assaulted him on the first step outside the Moon Gate from Anisbar to Vallazari. The Hidden Lands as a whole had a relatively temperate climate. These floating islands, which were home to the Ravela, were significantly warmer. A riot of birdsong filled the air, and the scent of spices drifted through the jungle greenery, reminding him of his early childhood in northern Ayana.

Galessel walked through the Moon Gate behind him and stopped, sniffing the air. Her hand entwined with his as she said, "I missed this place and its scents. It always reminds me of the kitchens during the Feast of the Goddess." She swatted at a large fly-like bug buzzing before her face. "But I didn't miss the insects."

Navarre smiled and squeezed her hand, feeling slightly disoriented. The ground beneath them moved ever so slightly, like a ship on a calm sea, reminding him they were on floating islands. What his body was feeling did not mesh with the lush jungle vista his eyes beheld, and it was making him nauseous.

"Come." Galessel pulled at his hand and started walking. "I tend to get seasick when I first arrive here. I find it helps to see the edge of where we're at. It gives the mind a reason for the body's motion."

Grateful for Galessel's empathy, he followed her, taking in the lush surroundings. Multi-hued, spiked flowers grew downward from palm tree-like plants with purple trunks and orange foliage. They walked a worn path through the jungle and stopped at an overlook with an edge protected by a rock rail.

The view took his breath away. Lush, jungle islands floated all around them, their rocky roots looking like inverted mountain tops. Rope bridges connected some of the closer islands, and a few of the bird-like Ravela danced in the air currents high above. Far below, nearly a mile by his estimate, was a vast body of water. Having been on high altitude airship voyages before, where the higher they went, the colder it became, Navarre found it puzzling that, this high above the water, it wasn't just warm, but hot.

The Hidden Lands were nothing if not an enigma.

On a nearby island, Navarre spotted a collection of curious buildings built, it seemed, haphazardly out of large branches and even the trunks of small trees. They looked curiously like giant bird's nests.

"It's beautiful, *ma chérie*," Navarre said. He wrapped his arm around Galessel, and she tucked her shoulder under his arm. "What are those buildings there?" He pointed toward the collection of nests.

"Those are the homes and common buildings of the Ravela. They're quite the engineering marvel." She sighed. "I wish we could linger. There is so much here I want to share with you, but time is of the essence. Since we cannot fly, we'll need to find a star-stone to take us to Vasyann."

Galessel turned back down the path, stopping when a small red-beaked, green and orange bird landed on her shoulder. It tweeted at her in a beautiful soprano voice.

Turning her head to look at the creature, she appeared to listen, then whistled a response when the bird stopped. Galessel and the bird went back and forth for several minutes.

Curiosity pulled Navarre to approach, but he kept his distance to avoid startling the bird.

After several more minutes of conversation, Galessel said, "Thank you so much little messenger." She reached into a pouch at her side, pulled something out and offered her open palm to the bird, which proceeded to eat what Navarre surmised to be seeds, before tweeting a short melody and flying off.

"What was that?" Navarre asked, joining Galessel back on the path.

"Keih, the little Queenfisher bird, is one of my family's messengers. She said the fionnaghs in Vallanon, Dunngrimm, and SoulScar have been saved, but there were some losses."

"What kind of losses?"

"Keih wasn't very clear—the poor things can't retain a lot of information and are really only used for short messages. But from what I could gather, we lost several soldiers and possibly a human." Galessel's eyes started to tear up. "But Keih didn't know who."

Navarre immediately quashed any thoughts of who they might have lost. Years of military training kicked in, letting him compartmentalize the information for later. He'd lost innumerable soldiers, and some good friends, in battle while serving in the Royal Guard. There'd be time to mourn when the mission was over.

He reached for Galessel's hand and wiped a tear from her cheek with his other hand. "Come *ma chérie*, it does us no good to worry for those who have passed. We must do our job so that we may save others from mourning."

Galessel nodded and led him farther into the jungle.

⊗ ⊗ ⊗

Navarre cut away a thick grey vine blocking their path. These islands were not hospitable to those who had to trek through the jungle. It was no wonder the Ravela developed the ability to fly. After a half-hour of walking, he wished he could.

He looked behind him to see how Galessel was doing. She trailed behind him only a little, giving him enough room to hack through the undergrowth. Her changed appearance still caught him off guard, but her eyes were the same, even when brimming with tears. She needed a distraction from thoughts of who they may have lost. He hoped through trying to satisfy his own curiosity, he could take her mind off of it. "Galessel, how is it that these islands float? Is it magic or some natural phenomenon?"

It took her a moment to reply. He wasn't sure if she'd been lost in thoughts or collecting them.

"The simple answer is magic. But as I know you will ask what kind, or how it came to be, I will tell you the story my grandmother told me when I was a child."

Once, a long time ago, there lived a tribe of peaceful folk called the Ravela. They loved all of the Hidden Lands' creatures, especially the birds. They befriended the many bird species on the islands, which at the time sat within the seas. They raised birds by hand and learned to communicate with them. After a while, the Ravela began to emulate the birds. They wore feathers and began building their homes to resemble bird nests. The Ravela lived in harmony with the birds and animals on the islands for many, many years.

Then, one day, a village was attacked by a giant bird that was unknown to the islanders. It was vulture-like, with long, sharp talons, a huge brutal beak, and bloody bones for wings. The bird attacked from in front of the sun, swooping down and snatching folk as it flew by. It would eat its victim in mid-flight, then streak down to grab another helpless villager. The Ravela tried to fend it off with spears and arrows, but its feathers were hard, providing it with armor, so their weapons had little effect on it. The survivors called it the Terror Bird.

As the attacks became more frequent, the Ravela became more desperate. They beseeched the gods, but no aid came. Finally King Savali'i and Queen Jiannisan made a promise to the gods that they would make any sacrifice to protect their people.

Vanriss, the goddess of nature, appeared before them and said, "I shall give you the means to protect your people from that which is an abomination in my eyes. The Terror Bird is not of my creation, but of Asher's. The sacrifice both of you must make is great. Do you truly wish to ask this of me?"

The king and queen both answered yes without hesitation.

As the gathered villagers watched, Vanriss moved her arms in a holy pattern that invoked the leaves of spring and tall oak trees in summer. Green light surrounded the king and queen until the light was too bright to look at. The villagers were forced to look away. When the light dimmed, the king and queen were gone, but in their place stood a beautiful blue and purple gryphon with wooden wings. The gryphon was taller than an old oak tree and looked down upon the Ravela with tears of compassion in its eyes. It said, "I am now called Soji, and I will protect you, and all of the Hidden Lands, forever."

Vanriss put her hand on the leg of the gryphon and said, "Because your sacrifice is timeless, you shall have the power of time in each violent breath. In every tear you shall have the power to restore that which has been damaged by violence."

Soji bowed to the goddess and took flight. The wind from its wings knocked folk from their feet. They watched as the gryphon soared high, and covered their ears when it shrieked its challenge to the Terror Bird.

It wasn't long before the monster answered with its own unworldly cry. Soon the sky was filled with shrieks and growls and thunder from the clash of the two creatures. Folk on the ground took cover as armored feathers fell from the sky, torn from the Terror Bird by Soji's golden claws. The battle raged for hours, and blood rained from the sky in great drops.

When finally, the Terror Bird fell from the sky, Soji landed near it and breathed a breath like fog over it. Before the villagers' eyes, the horrible bird decayed into a pile of dust and blew away.

Spent, but not yet done with its task, Soji sunk to the ground and told the folk to bring any who had been injured by the Terror Bird. For each one, Soji cried a single tear, healing them of any wounds. When the task was done, Soji, in a dual, harmonic voice, said, "I shall always come to your aid should you need me, my children." The great gryphon then flew high into the sky, until it could no longer be seen.

All was well for a time, but the Ravela dearly missed their rulers, so they prayed to Vanriss yet again. When the goddess appeared, they pleaded with her. "Please, great Vanriss, we miss our rulers. They are so very far away from us. Can you bring them back to us and make them Ravela again?"

Vanriss was thoughtful for a moment. With sadness in her voice, she answered, "No. What has been done cannot be undone. Your king and queen made a sacrifice, and to undo it would bring the Terror Bird back, and possibly something even worse." The goddess smiled. "But what I can do is bring you closer to Soji."

The goddess raised her arms, and all of the islands of Vallazari and Vasyann rose from the sea and began to float in the air. But they did not rise high enough. Vanriss looked puzzled. Nothing she did raised the islands any higher.

A small girl said, "Perhaps our sorrow weighs so heavily upon us that the islands are too heavy."

Vanriss thought about that for a while and then said, "Since you have taken such good care of my birds, I shall make your bones as hollow as theirs so that your homes shall be among the clouds and thus, closer to Soji." Vanriss snapped her fingers and all of the Ravela became as light as birds. And because their bones were now so much lighter, the islands began to rise into the clouds.

When the first islands rose through the clouds, Soji flew to greet them, telling Vanriss, "We are filled with joy to see our people again. Thank you, Vanriss. We are grateful for your kindness. We will live our life to honor you."

With this, Vanriss was pleased, and she said, "Then I will leave you with one last gift. I shall teach your people to fly."

The Ravela began to change. Feathers sprouted from their skin, their heads became more bird-like, and they grew wings upon their backs. When their feathers were done growing, the young ones started flapping their new wings, and took to the air as if they'd been flying all their lives. The older folk were more hesitant, but after a time, even they could not resist trying their new skills.

"And that's how the Ravela came to be and the islands began to float." Galessel concluded.

Navarre had been so drawn in by Galessel's tale he was surprised to note, at some point in the story, they'd quit walking. He was even more surprised to find they'd been surrounded by Ravela. Folk of every color and varying feather patterns were seated cross-legged around them, seemingly as enthralled by Galessel's tale as he was.

One of the Ravela stood and bowed to Galessel. She had the feathers of a hawk around her head but the iridescent black of the raven over her body. When she spoke, her voice was high but harsh, a blend again of the two birds. "Your tale was well told and truthful in every way. How is it a human knows our story so well?"

Galessel seemed taken aback but then recovered. She must have forgotten about her disguise. "My mother gave me the gift of your tale, and I have remembered it always. It was one of my favorites." She paused for a moment. "How she knew of it, I know not. Perhaps my grandmother heard it from a satyr in her younger years."

The Ravela smiled. "Then all blessings upon your mother, fair human. What brings you to Vallazari?"

"We have come to warn Soji that they are in grave danger. There are humans who have come to the Hidden Lands to destroy the fionnagh, and Soji with them."

"That is troubling news, human. I must confer with my people. If you will excuse us."

The hawk-raven Ravela gathered her people around her at the edge of the clearing. To Navarre's ears their discourse sounded like a group of parrots speaking, though he could not understand their language.

"Do you think they will help us, or hinder us, *ma chérie?*"

Galessel, intent on listening in on the Ravelas' discussion took a moment to respond. "I haven't had much reason to interact with the Ravela before, so my translation skills are rusty, but I think they will help us." She entwined her hand in his. "Should they decide otherwise, I may have the means to convince them to at least let us pass unharmed."

Navarre wondered at what she meant, but didn't press, figuring it was something magical or possibly a negotiation tactic he was unaware of. He watched the Ravela in fascination.

They were a curious folk, and Navarre surmised the crows of Ashelon, were they to be made more human, would be very much like the Ravela, with their delicate chain ornaments and necklaces of shiny bits and bobs. They wore no clothes, being protected by feathers, but some had colorful strips of fabric tied around their ankles.

After a few minutes, the Ravela returned. "We have decided to help you. You may be human, but no one who wishes us ill would have told our story with such passion. But the true test will be if you know the song for the stone. Please, follow us." The hawk-raven Ravela gestured down a faint path with her wing.

Navarre and Galessel proceeded down the path with the flock of Ravela in tow.

⚙ ⚙ ⚙

The star-stone sat in the center of a volcanic rock-rimmed clearing, not far from where they'd met the

Ravela. In spite of its closeness, Navarre and Galessel never would have found it on their own. The jungle was thick, and the path branched out in several false trails.

Navarre held back while Galessel approached the white marble pillar. Runes, inlaid with some kind of red stone, stood in rows upon it. Before it, Galessel sang a song in elvish. Navarre's elvish was getting better, but Galessel sang so softly he couldn't make out the words. As she finished the song, three runes began to glow with an orange light.

Galessel touched each one, starting with the top rune, working downward. She then stepped back as a shimmering silver doorway appeared in front of the stone. The Ravela all made soft clicking noises.

"Shall we?" Galessel asked Navarre.

They stepped through together.

Stepping through the doorway felt like walking through cold spiderwebs. Navarre shivered, fighting the urge to brush unseen webs from his arms. Galessel, and the flock of Ravela who followed them through, didn't seem to have the same reaction to the passage. Maybe the doorway only affected humans?

The air was cooler here, and breathing felt a little harder, leading Navarre to surmise they were even higher than the previous islands. They'd come through to a gigantic coliseum, rivaling the size of the ancient one in Roma. This one had four tiers, each with forty-foot tall doorways spaced every two hundred feet or so. It looked to be made of ancient marble but was in much better condition than its Roman counterpart.

A shadow moved across the floor of the coliseum, followed by a substantial rush of air and the whooshing sound of gigantic wings. A giant gryphon landed in the center of the coliseum, touching down as if it weighed no more than a cavalry horse.

Navarre was struck with awe. The gryphon was enormous, towering at least seventy-five feet above them as it sat like a cat, with a purple-furred tail curled around gold-taloned feet. Blue feathers covered the gryphon's head, shoulders, and the base of the wine-red, wooden wings. Soji's eyes flashed gold, matching its beak.

Curiously, a glowing blue fairy lamp hung from the gryphon's neck on a thick bronze chain.

Without preamble, Soji spoke. "Whom do you serve?" Soji's voice was as Galessel described it—two voices in perfect harmony—but there would have been no way for her to capture the beauty of the duality of the male and female voices speaking simultaneously.

Galessel stepped forward, her hands stiff at her sides as if she was trying not to clench them in fear or nervousness, or both. "We, Navarre and I, serve the Hidden Lands, great Soji."

"And who are you, elf maid?"

The Ravela started chittering amongst themselves. Navarre wondered how the gryphon knew the truth of Galessel's race but shrugged it off. Who knew what kind of powers a gods-created creature had?

"I am Princess Galessel of the Anisbarii Court—she who has been branded *sikevra*."

The Ravela gathered around them gasped in unison, sounding like a flock of angry geese.

"If the gods themselves have spurned you, what makes you so arrogant, and so foolish, as to think that I will hear you? I should eat you and your companion before Vanriss herself punishes us for even letting you live." Soji loomed over them.

Navarre moved his hand to the hilt of his rapier, but Galessel's hand on his arm caused him to pause. She flashed him a look before answering the gryphon.

"I beg for your restraint, great Soji. I know we have no right to be here in your presence and that by being here, we're putting you and the Ravela in danger. Were the need not so dire, and the danger not so near, we would not be here. I am merely the third daughter of the House of Anisbar, but I come with a warning. A group of humans called the Hammer Guardians are on their way here to destroy the fionnagh, and you with it. Though I am a mere elf, I would give my life in exchange for your help in stopping them."

Navarre added, "As would I," and dropped to one knee before the gryphon. Galessel followed suit.

Soji looked at Galessel. "You have the gift. You could have forced me to aid you."

"It is not my wish to force you to do anything. You vowed long ago to come to the defense of the Hidden Lands. I come before you today to humbly beg for your help in defending my people and all of the Hidden Lands."

The gryphon snorted, clawing the ground with its talons. Navarre's hand went to his sword hilt once again, unsure of what Galessel had said to anger Soji.

"How touching," a brusk male voice said from behind Navarre. "You may fire when ready."

Chapter 13
Vasyann

Navarre tackled Galessel, shielding her from the barrage of bullets that seemed to come from everywhere. He felt the passing of one bullet over his shoulder and heard several shots ricochet off of Soji's wooden wings. The screams of injured Ravela echoed through the coliseum, an eerie, raucous sound that set Navarre's nerves even more on edge.

With a quick glance, Navarre assessed the situation. Four Ravela were slowly, painfully dissolving near the star stone, victims of cold-iron. At least nine Hammer Guardians surrounded them. Some were reloading, while two others were carrying a lead box away. They were lucky the Hammer Guardians weren't a well-organized military force, or they'd all be dead right now.

As a short man with a black handlebar mustache fumbled with his sidearm and drew his sword, Navarre saw an opening. He rolled forward, coming up in a lunge, his sword running the short man through. It was a painful, slow-killing blow, but it was enough. The short man dropped to his knees, his hands gripping his stomach.

Stepping back from his lunge, Navarre faced off before two more Hammer Guardians, who rushed him with rapiers high, hoping to take him while he was off balance. Except that he wasn't. It would take more than two subpar sword wielders to take him down. He swatted aside the dark man's overhead strike as he would a pesky fly and kicked the chestnut-haired woman square in the face. She reeled back, blood running from her nose, her eyes slightly glassy. Navarre connected his left fist with the man's solar plexus, and as the Hammer Guardian doubled over, followed with an upward slash across his throat.

Two down.

The woman screamed, rushing Navarre and swinging her sword wildly, her pistol forgotten at her side. He parried her clumsy attempt to slash his throat, and with a perfect riposte, sunk his blade into her heart. As she fell away from his blade, Navarre looked for Galessel.

Navarre shook his head, unsure if he'd been struck without realizing it. The scene before him seemed out of a dream. Galessel was surrounded by three Hammer Guardians: one incredibly tall and slim, a stout one in a bowler hat who seemed familiar, and a woman with flame-orange hair. All three moved as if slowed by tar, while Galessel danced with unnatural quickness, even for an elf. Her face held a look of grim satisfaction as she moved through her three opponents, hitting each with a series of precise strikes to the wrists—a move Navarre called "the hornet's sting." The weapons of all three Hammer Guardians dropped from their hands, the tendons in their wrists severed.

"Yield," Galessel commanded. There was a quality to her voice that Navarre had never heard before. All three dropped to their knees, whimpering in pain.

The coliseum was suddenly filled with the harmonic roar of two lions. Navarre looked toward the sound. Soji stood, wings held high, and did something he'd never seen another being do.

Soji breathed a cone of purple and black energy at three Hammer Guardians who'd been trying to sneak behind the gryphon. As the energy washed over them, they froze, looking terrified. Within moments, they started to age rapidly. All had been in their twenties, maybe early thirties, but now, they looked to be eighty or older. The two holding the lead box dropped it, their fingers suddenly unable to hold it any longer. Even after the energy dissipated, they continued to age, their skin becoming thin and spotted, then flaking from their bodies as they crumbled to dust.

With the same disdain a cat would give a dead mouse, Soji turned from the pile of dust and focused their attention on Galessel.

Navarre followed Soji's gaze. Galessel was angrier than he'd ever seen her, but scared as well. Her hands were clenched at her sides and the redness in her cheeks stood out against the unusual pallor of her skin. Her voice shook as she stared down the last of the invaders.

"For all that you have done to my people, I should let Soji slay you where you stand. For the evil you represent, I should mount your skulls on spikes as a warning to Queen Victoria. As long as there are good people left in the world, both fae and human, we shall never surrender to her tyranny, and we will never stop resisting her. Her brand of evil will not gain a foothold here."

The one in the bowler hat spat on the ground and squared his shoulders. Navarre recognized him, now that he was holding still, as Kane, the leader of the Hammer Guardians. He'd seen the bulbous-nosed brute on a wanted poster years ago.

Kane smirked at Galessel. "Tell that to all of those pony abominations, you stupid fly. Those fleabags screamed and winked right out of existence. And you know what we did? We laughed—was the best day of our lives. I can't wait to see the look on your faces when all of your feeon-whatevers are destroyed! Queen Victoria's army will march right over the ashes and rule this putrid, Asher-forsaken land."

Navarre stepped forward, his arm raised to club Kane senseless but a look from Galessel stalled him. He lowered his arm but stayed ready to move at a glance from her.

Galessel smiled, but it didn't reach her eyes. It was, Navarre was afraid to admit, scary. "Then this really isn't your day. You may have destroyed the land and beings of Alexandria, but the rest of the fionnaghs are safe. Your plan has been foiled. You and your remaining soldiers will be punished for what you've done."

With that pronouncement, the other two Hammer Guardians slumped, the fight gone from them. Kane was not so easily cowed. "Do your worst. We are not afraid of death, *fly*!"

"All the more reason for you to live and face judgement for your crimes." Galessel motioned for the Ravela to take the prisoners away.

Navarre watched as the Ravela tied up the humans and lifted them into the air. They didn't fly far—just over to the next floating island. Other Ravela flew on to land on a shelf of rock which jutted from the root of the island.

Within moments, rope and wood cages hung from the rock, their doors open. With seemingly practiced ease, the Ravela swung and then flung their charges into the cages and locked the doors. Even if the humans did manage to escape, there was nowhere to go but down. Nearly a mile down to the ocean. Mere mortals couldn't survive that drop. And above them, the rock appeared sheer enough to prevent climbing.

Navarre wondered at the ready availability of the cages so near the coliseum and decided he really didn't want to know what kinds of things took place there.

Soji's harmonic voice pulled him back to face the gryphon. "Those humans destroyed a fionnagh and murdered citizens of the Hidden Lands. They deserved to be executed. You are too soft, highness."

Galessel faced the gryphon, grim determination on her face. Only a slight tremor in her hands betrayed her fear. What she said next, Navarre was not expecting. "My ear tips were cut off by the Svellvega, which branded me *sikevra* by default and exiled me without a trial. I would not see anyone else suffer consequences without the benefit of having justice done. Regardless of the fate that has befallen me, I choose the path of compassion."

Without warning, Soji reared back and let loose their breath on Galessel, covering her in purple-black light.

"No!" Navarre ran toward Galessel, intending to pull her from the aging light. But he was too late. Soji's breath ceased. As Navarre's eyes cleared from the after-burn of the light, Galessel stood before him, shaking and her makeup gone, but otherwise whole.

Soji bowed before Galessel, bending one foreleg in supplication. "Forgive me, your highness, but it was the only way to test the truth of your words. Only one who is innocent in the eyes of the gods is immune to my breath."

Navarre rushed to Galessel and pulled her to him. The cinnamon scent of her skin was reassuring, as were the tears that leaked from her violet eyes. "Let's not do that again, *ma chérie*. Next time, warn me that you are safe from such magics."

Galessel buried her face in his chest. "I didn't know."

Chapter 14
Death's Embrace

With the last of the humans left to their fate, Murik adjusted *Death's Embrace's* heading toward the Sun Gate that hovered over the sea east of the floating islands of Vallazari and Vasyann. With any luck, he'd make it through before the Hidden Lands fell apart from the destruction of the fionnaghs.

Not that he cared one way or the other. The engines were set at a leisurely speed. If the Svellvega vanished, and he with them, then so be it. That was the goal, after all.

A small voice in his mind wondered if he'd truly disappear, or just half of him. He was a half-breed, the product of a Svellvega father and an Anisbarii elf mother.

His father was Kanayda, a renowned pirate captain, one of the only ones to successfully raid deep into Anisbarii territory, from which he stole an Anisbarii elf maid. To this day, Murik didn't know why Kanayda kept Murik's mother alive or why his father allowed her to carry a half-breed to term. Maybe it was simply due to a lack of concern, or lack time at the homestead, for when he returned from one of his many raids to find the elf maid had delivered a son, he stabbed her through the heart for the sole crime of shedding tears and threw her body into the sea.

Kanayda promptly returned to his ship, leaving Murik to die. Except that Murik didn't.

When Kanayda returned, days later, Murik was still alive. So his father gave him his name, which meant "refuse" or "garbage," and handed him off to a series of female captives to raise. His father never acknowledged him as a son, treating him as a slave, and even worse, never truly acknowledging his existence.

When Murik was about five years old, talk began to spread in their small village about how he was beginning to resemble his father. Bastard children were not of much consequence to the Svellvega, but talk also started to arise about how Murik's ears were too short and his skin too dark.

It was becoming obvious he was a half-breed. Kanayda could have killed him then but chose not to. Instead, he loaded Murik onto his ship and flew to the land of Rondahar, where he sold him to the mountain trolls.

Truth be told, Kanayda did him a favor when he sold him off. Sure, the mountain trolls worked him like the slave he was, but in his off time, he learned as much as he could. He skulked around the shipyards, learning what he could from the shadows, fought with other slaves in the fighting pits, and generally soaked up knowledge wherever he could find it, including the art of blood magic.

He made few friends and was never really accepted by anyone. It didn't matter. He found comfort, when it suited him, in the arms of the pit fighters he hadn't managed to defeat, and the rest of the time, his anger kept him company.

When Murik turned twenty, he left the mountain trolls, finding it surprisingly easy to blood-bond himself to a ship and sail away. The trolls treated their slaves rather well and most elected to stay, but those who wished to leave after ten years of service were allowed to go—he'd spent fifteen. He knew the trolls wouldn't miss him.

As he'd sailed away from Rondahar, he'd vowed to get revenge on his father. He spent the next decade systematically hunting and eradicating his father's offspring. Twenty-three siblings fell to his blade, each adding to his reputation as a ruthless scourge of the skies.

When he finally returned to DawnGuard, some twenty-five years after being taken away by his father, he'd half hoped his father would welcome him home and recognize him as his only son and heir.

He was a fool for having even that half hope. Kanayda had laughed in his face. Murik drew his cutlass and challenged his father to single combat.

It didn't take long for word to spread, and soon a group of Svellvega was gathered around the pair outside Kanayda's homestead. In the weak light of the northern spring, Kanayda had looked nothing like the swaggering pirate he'd been when Murik was young. The elder Svellvega was haggard, his white hair thinning and tangled, and his beard unkempt. Dark circles ringed his eyes and his breath stank of the strong spirits from the tribes of the far, far north.

Disappointment dulled the spark of Murik's revenge. He'd found no challenge before him. His father was a pitiful shell of the elf he once was. Once the circle was drawn around them in the sand, Murik had stood, waiting. His father bellowed in defiance and stepped toward him.

"Once I would have done anything to make you proud of me, but now, you are nothing to me." Murik held out his fist toward his father.

Kanayda gasped as blood oozed from his pores, slowly at first, then built into thick streams which flew through the air, and collected around Murik's fist.

With a flourish, Murik had opened his fist and the blood splashed to the ground. Kanayda crumpled, nothing more than a dried out husk. That was the beauty of blood magic. Normally it required the use of one's own blood or of someone else, but when you shared blood with someone, it was so easy to use it against them.

Murik had faced the assembled crowd, noting the looks of fear and surprise many wore. He'd grinned.

"I am Murik, bastard son of Kanayda. I have killed all of my siblings, and I claim, by Svellvegan law, all that Kanayda owned: his house, his ship, his slaves, and his rank of captain. Does anyone oppose me?" No one spoke. "Then it is done. From this day until my last, I will be known as Captain Murik."

The watching crowd had disbursed, leaving behind one well-dressed noble. He was striking in his appearance, and Murik had felt an instant attraction. The noble approached and said, "Greetings, Captain. I am Lord

Davorin. I could use an elf of your particular talents. I can give you a fleet of ships to command, all the wealth you desire and power. So much power. What say you?"

Murik had looked the lord over. It wasn't every day someone made such a generous offer. But what was his angle? He'd quickly decided that it didn't matter. He'd had his revenge and wasn't sure what to do. And the lord was handsome. "Sure, why not."

It wasn't long before their relationship developed into something more personal. After that, it was easy to bind Davorin to him. Murik was the only one Davorin trusted with a razor, and since he eschewed body hair, Murik had ample opportunity for a slip of the razor here and there to gather blood.

He supposed he could have loved Davorin, but can you really love someone you have complete dominion over? In the end, Davorin had been nothing more than a useful tool.

Murik wasn't sure he'd be alive much longer either. It didn't really matter.

The sound of thunder startled him from his journey down the halls of memory. As his vision focused on the present, the view from the wheelhouse filled with the backlit silhouette of a ship coming at him out of the Sun Gate.

Before he could react, several explosions knocked him off his feet. A shudder passed along his heart from his blood connection to the ship. He could tell *Death's Embrace* would soon live up to its name. The ship was crippled, the lower engines gone. The only things keeping it in the sky were the neolithium-filled balloon and the hydronium-powered sails. A hit to either would send him tumbling from the sky.

"Surrender and prepare to be boarded, you bastard!"

Murik stood to find a sylph with red-tinged wings flying about twenty feet away, aiming two rather large pistols at his head. He had heard about N'hena, the fierce sylph captain, and had, in fact, attacked her ship, *The Intrepid*, but he'd never actually seen her before.

He thought about giving her an obscene finger gesture as his last act of defiance, but his ego wouldn't allow for that. It would be an incredibly anti-climactic way to die—and he'd done so much in his life that was more worthy of a different end.

He raised his hands high and said, "Very well. I surrender." Through his blood bond, he activated the ship's wards. He wouldn't give up his ship that easily.

The Intrepid lowered to match altitude and sent their gangplank over. As Murik started across, he had a brief moment of weakness. He could just end it here. Walk off the gangplank and fall a mile or so to the ocean. He looked down and saw Ravela flying below him, waiting for just such a maneuver. They really wanted him alive.

So be it. They would regret it.

The moment he stepped foot on *The Intrepid*, he was pulled around and relieved of his weapons. His hands were bound, as were his ankles, and he was pushed to the deck. A solid kick to his side forced him to roll onto his back. The crew looked ready to murder him on the spot, especially the tarted up faun in brown and white striped short trousers and pomegranate red blouse.

Her metal hooves thunked on the deck as she approached. Looming over him, she said, "Galessel is really looking forward to seeing you again."

Murik met her gaze. "Ah, she's that little Anisbarii tramp who's ears I trimmed, right?" He laughed as the faun's ears laid back against her head. "Isn't she *sikevra* now? I wouldn't mind collecting that bounty. After this, I could use a little spending money." He laughed even harder as the faun slowly raised one metal foot above his face.

Before she could stomp the life from him, a dark, meaty fellow, half-giant from the look of his flattened nose and shortened, pointed ears, pulled her back, nearly lifting her off her feet. "Why don't you take some of the crew over to search his ship," the half-giant said.

The faun nodded and the lout let her go. He shouldn't have. Murik could see the fury boiling behind her eyes. She walked away from Murik and turned back abruptly. The last thing he saw before darkness engulfed him was a polished steel hoof heading right at his face.

MURiK

Chapter 15
Death's Embrace

Kicking Murik in the face felt good. Clove knew she shouldn't have, but she couldn't help herself. That pirate had maimed her best friend and clearly would do it again if he could.

Once on the deck of Murik's ship, she made every effort to stomp across the wood planking, leaving a trail of hoof marks. She heard N'hena snicker above her.

"Clove, be careful, there's probably cold-iron all over that ship. Point stuff out to the humans, but keep your distance, all right?" N'hena yelled down from near the bottom of the balloon. Her smaller size meant any cold-iron would affect her faster than most of the other fae on her ship, but it didn't mean she couldn't do recon from the air.

Clove nodded as she headed toward the stairs that would lead to the belly of the ship. She followed behind several of N'hena's human crew, unhappy about not being in the lead, but willing, this time, to let them. Cold-iron bullets weren't an instant death sentence to them, and they had no idea if Murik was alone on his ship or not.

Surprisingly, they found no one down below. The ship was empty but for one large crate that held an enormous cold-iron bomb and a few smaller crates of ammunition.

Clove headed back topside, not willing to test how close she could get to cold-iron without becoming ill. The humans were more than capable of inventorying what was left. One thing did puzzle her though. Why hadn't Murik used the cold-iron bomb on Soji? Wouldn't that be the most effective use of such a thing, given the threat Soji posed? Unless... Unless he was going to use it on the Anisbarii palace instead.

The bastard seemed to have a death wish, so destroying the palace would net him greater destruction, and then it wouldn't matter if Soji destroyed him after. The thought made her shiver.

Clove placed a hoof on the second stair to the deck and heard a soft click. She sprung forward, but not fast enough. Something shot from the wall, piercing her back just under her ribs then withdrawing. Her kidney erupted in a fiery blaze of pain and she screamed. Stars impeded her vision as she fell forward onto the deck. She tried to rise, but any movement sent waves of pain through her back.

She heard N'hena above her barking orders, but couldn't find the strength to raise her head. Whatever she'd been hit with must have had cold-iron in it.

"You lot, take this ship through the Sun Gate along with a flock of Ravela. Blow some more holes in the hull, tear up the sails, and shred the balloon. Let this piece of cold-iron-filled junk sink in Ashelon. The Ravela will fly you back here. We'll rendezvous at the palace in Anisbar."

There was a short pause in N'hena's orders, and Clove felt the breeze of N'hena's wings above her. "And you—help me get Clove back aboard *The Intrepid*. Goddess help her, she's been pierced by cold-iron."

Cold flowed from her back through her limbs, and Clove started to shiver. Was this what dying felt like? She tried to move, but her legs wouldn't respond. Her vision narrowed to a black field with pinpricks of light, and her ears felt stuffed with oliphant wool. As if from a great distance, she felt herself being picked up, and then the world ceased to exist.

clove

Chapter 16
Anisbar

The royal palace in Anisbar was a hive of controlled chaos. Navarre held Galessel's hand as they ran behind the elves carrying Clove to the herbalist's wing. Worry creased Galessel's forehead, but she was holding up well. They'd returned just after some of N'hena's crew had come through the gate with Clove.

He'd seen a cohort of guards escorting a badly beaten Svellvegan elf to the dungeons but hadn't gotten the chance to find out what that was all about. Their focus had been immediately taken by Clove's dire situation. Navarre knew someone would fill him in on pertinent information when he needed to know. Right now he needed to be here for Galessel.

Tensions were high in the palace. They ran past guards stationed at every corridor, and a brief glance out a window showed him ranks upon ranks of soldiers on the palace grounds. The Anisbarii were preparing for war.

Navarre smelled the earthiness of the herbalist's wing before they took a sharp left at the end of the hall. As they rounded the corner, he nearly collided with an elf carrying a crate that smelled strongly of ginger. Their progress was further hampered by a phalanx of several physicians, nurses, and what he assumed was an alchemist, in bright green robes and black-lensed goggles, carrying a box of glass bottles, all heading toward the palace gates.

Navarre looked to Galessel as they stepped aside to let two burly elves carrying a stack of litters pass them.

"What did we come back to?" Navarre asked.

Galessel shrugged. "Judging from what I've seen so far, Father's preparing for an attack. I can send for news once we find out what's wrong with Clove."

Navarre nodded and followed Galessel into a circular room with a glass ceiling. The space was roughly divided in half with one side containing beds arranged along the walls, each separated by woven fiber screens painted with bright landscapes. The other half looked more like a treatment area. There were fewer beds, and each was paired with a large porcelain wash basin, topped with a water spigot, and several tables filled with a variety of medical instruments, many of which were unfamiliar to Navarre. Above each bed hung a large lamp. Most were shuttered, but the one above the table where Clove lay face down was unshuttered, allowing a pure white light to shine over the table.

Galessel dropped Navarre's hand and rushed to her friend's side. She picked up Clove's unresponsive hand and tears filled her eyes but did not spill. "What happened to her?" she demanded.

The elf who replied was dressed in simple grey loose pants and a fitted tunic. Navarre presumed she was the healer.

"She only just got here, Princess, but from what I've been told, it's likely she's been exposed to cold-iron. Now give me some room, and let me tend to my patient."

Spinning her long brown braid into a bun at the back of her head, and pulling the end through to knot it, the healer washed her hands in the basin before picking up a pair of scissors and cutting away Clove's bloody shirt.

An assistant, dressed in a similar grey uniform, used a sea sponge to wipe away blackened blood and a sickly green substance from Clove's back. The exposed wound looked to be a jagged puncture from something fairly large.

Navarre moved closer but was careful to stay out of the healer's way. The skin around the wound was puckered and mottled with patches of bright red and an almost mustard yellow. He'd seen enough wounds turn gangrenous on the battlefield to know Clove was in serious danger. If whatever had pierced her back had hit her kidney, she didn't have long.

He returned to Galessel and put his hand on her back. She leaned into him briefly, but never took her attention from Clove.

The healer, donning an odd pair of prism-lensed glasses, inspected the damage, her nose an inch from the wound. After a moment, she straightened and removed the glasses. "This was definitely caused by cold-iron."

She looked at Galessel. "I'm sorry, Princess, we don't have anything that can treat a wound like this. All I can do is give her something to ease the suffering, but I'm afraid it's only a matter of time. I'm actually quite surprised that she's not dead already."

Navarre gave the healer credit for not mincing words. He valued a no-nonsense assessment, but he could tell by Galessel's trembling she hadn't taken the news well. "Your bedside manner needs some work, doctor."

The healer looked him in the eye. "Would you rather I lie and tell the princess that everything will be all right? By the look of you, I'd guess you're that human soldier the king is so fond of. Navarre, is it? You should be used to a straightforward manner."

Navarre started to reply, but Galessel interrupted. "If there's nothing you can do, send for my grandmother. She'll know of something."

The elven doctor's eyes softened. "I can send for her, Princess, but she will tell you the same thing I have. There is no cure for cold-iron poisoning. Unless you can bring back the black lilies, but they've been extinct for almost two hundred years."

Galessel stiffened under Navarre's hand and her eyes went wide. She started going through her pouches, pulling out items and dropping them to the floor until she found what she was looking for. Her eyes lit up as she held out a small crystallized black lily. "Will this work?" she asked.

The doctor's eyes never left the flower as she carefully took the lily from Galessel's outstretched hand. "Where did you get this?"

"From my grandmother," Galessel replied. "She gave it to me when I was assigned to Ashelon as our ambassador." There was an edge of smugness to her voice.

The healer bowed her head briefly. "Thank you, Princess. You may have just saved your friend's life. Now give me room to work."

The elf cupped the lily in her hands and whispered something Navarre didn't understand. The flower uncrystallized and grew under the healer's breath. She plucked two petals and several of the stamens and handed the remains to her assistant. "Put the rest in a stasis bottle and put the bottle in the cabinet of rare cures. Pray to the Goddess we won't need what's left."

The assistant nodded and ran to do the healer's bidding. Meanwhile, Navarre watched with rapt attention while the elf rubbed the flower pieces in her hand, turning them into a black paste.

She packed the paste into the wound, then stood back, waiting. Clove woke suddenly, arching in pain as a yellow pus flecked with rust iron oozed from the wound. Galessel did her best to comfort Clove.

"You, Navarre, if you'd be so kind as to clean the wound? The lily's magic is said to neutralize cold-iron, but I cannot take that chance if I'm to be of service during the war."

Navarre did as ordered, wondering at the speed with which the jagged edges of Clove's wound were closing. Before his eyes, the hole closed, and Clove sagged back down, this time asleep, her breathing even and slow.

His hands full of bloody, gross rags, Navarre looked to the doctor for what to do with them. She pointed to a lead box in a corner.

"We don't deal with cold-iron much, but that box will do for disposal for now." The elf washed her hands in the basin once again and began applying a salve to Clove's back. "I'll need to keep her here for a few days while she regains her strength, but I believe the danger is over. Congratulations, your highness, you've saved your friend's life, and possibly many others with that black lily."

Tears ran down Galessel's face. She still held on to Clove's hand. "Healer Siora, while I am very happy to have helped, it was Clove that hung on to life so fiercely. Any other fae would have been dead in minutes, if not seconds. How did she hold on for so long?"

"Your guess is as good as mine, your highness. It could have been that the weapon was only painted with cold-iron, or it's possible that her time in Ashelon allowed her to build up somewhat of an immunity. It helped that whatever did this didn't stay in her body."

As he washed his hands in the basin, Navarre said, "Please forgive my earlier harshness, Healer. It has been a stressful day."

"Just as I am straightforward with my assessments, I also know not to take personally the responses or attitudes of my patients' friends and family. I understand the stress and pain you must be going through—especially after the loss of your other companion. I should have been more compassionate."

The memory of the message about one of their companions being killed flashed through his mind. "Oh no. We heard vague news earlier but not word on who it was. Who did we lose?" Navarre had a sinking feeling in his chest.

Galessel pulled a blanket over Clove's sleeping form and came to stand by his side.

The healer's face was pained. "Oh, I'm sorry. I thought you knew. Your companion Morgan fell to one of the

Hammer Guardians. She died saving the D'zur. Word tells, she shielded the cold-iron from them with her own body." She paused. "I'm so sorry for your loss. May her name be ever on the wind and her heart with the Goddess."

The world disappeared. Images of Morgan flashed through his mind. Nights spent drinking after guard duty, betting on who would woo the barmaid on any given night, crazy adventures and battles alike. Morgan was more than his lieutenant, more than a staunch ally and boon companion, she was his best friend.

And she was gone. Gone forever.

His legs lost their strength, and he sat heavily on the floor. Covering his face with his hands, he wept. After a few moments, Galessel sat beside him cradling his head. He felt her crying with him and held her to him.

Chapter 17
Anisbar

Galessel tried to calm her racing heart. Navarre squeezed her hand, and she looked at him, grateful to have him at her side. They stood, surrounded by palace guards, behind her mother, grandmother, and father, in the great hall, hidden from the assembled crowd. Her sisters stood to one side of them, flanked by a rank of palace guards. On the other side were her boon companions, Samga and Eirsal, both clad in mourning grey like Navarre. Clove was still in the healing wing, recovering.

The tension was so thick Galessel found it hard to breathe. Members of nearly every race in the Hidden

Lands filled the cavernous hall. The absence of the centaurs was noted by a space in the ranks of the fae assembled. Representatives from the Seelie and Unseelie courts stood opposite each other, as did the Svellvegan queen with her elite troops, and equal number of Anisbarii soldiers headed by General Ilvisar. The murmuring of the assembled host began to build as they waited for her mother to speak.

When Queen Thessalia finally stepped forward, the noise from the crowd fell away. Her mother's ability to command a room without speaking always left Galessel with a sense of awe.

"Thank you all for attending this emergency council, especially Queen Kaneti and her assembled armies. We stand on the brink of war, but what has happened in our realms affects us all and should be reason for us to band together, not engage in conflict. Some of you know, but many do not, of the cause of the recent earthquake and the disappearance of the centaur and nightsteeds. I am sad to report that both races are gone, wiped from existence by the destruction of the Alexandrian fionnagh."

The crowd gasped in collective horror. Questions shouted from many beings combined into a cacophony of noise. Thessalia held up her hands for silence, and eventually the crowd fell quiet. "We have found the ones responsible, and if not for the bravery and sacrifice of a few, we all would have suffered the same fate. We bring before you the ones who attempted to destroy the Hidden Lands."

The three Hammer Guardians that Galessel and Navarre apprehended were brought forward in chains. They all looked battered, sunburned, and bug-eaten. Their week in the Ravela's cages had not been pleasant. Behind them, surrounded by additional guards, was Murik. Hatred glowed in his bruised eyes as he looked at the assembled fae.

Galessel's mother continued, her voice lower with power and purpose. "We give the humans to the Unseelie Court, the Seelie Court, and the D'zur to execute justice and blood price for their crimes. Crimes that include invading our realm, genocide of two of our races, multiple murders, and poisoning our lands and people with cold-iron."

The crowd erupted in screams of anger and insults directed at the humans. For a small instant, Galessel felt sorry for them. But that pity was quashed the minute she looked over at Samga and Navarre. Morgan and countless others were gone. All for greed and hatred.

Each of the human prisoners was taken to the named courts. The Seelie king, Oberon, an equal in height and stature to Damháin, but fair of skin with hair the color of sunflowers, put his prisoner to her knees, and she was immediately surrounded by lavender-skinned pixies armed with wickedly serrated knives.

"We shall devise brave punishments for thee, vile knave," the king declared.

Damháin of the Unseelie brought his massive club down on the head of his prisoner, splattering the surrounding fae with blood and brains. The Anisbarii guards backed away quickly, wiping ichor from their armor.

The last human scrambled and fought his guards as they dragged him, screaming, to the D'zur. Spinel Opalforged forced him to his knees and pulled his head back by his hair, saying, "You will work in the mines until the blood price is paid—or you die."

Queen Kaneti of the Svellvega, resplendent in a red dress, stepped forward to address Thessalia. "And what of Murik? My spies informed me he was the one who led these humans in an attempt to destroy us all. I give you my word, as a fellow queen, his punishment will last for days."

The crowd yelled their approval. Fae of all races stomped the floor or banged on armor and shields. Galessel fought to keep her hands at her side and not covering her ears, it was so loud.

Thessalia once again held up her hands for silence. The crowd obeyed. "Murik shares the crimes of the Hammer Guardians to be sure, but he has committed one additional grave and tragic crime for which he must answer for." She stepped aside and motioned for Galessel to step forward.

Galessel had known what to expect when she stepped before the crowd, her ears undisguised, but the hisses, boos, and insults still hit her like fists to the gut.

"*Sikevra!*" one of Damháin's goblins cried, pointing at her. The Unseelie king, staring daggers at her from the front of the crowd, smacked his club into his hand several times, causing blood droplets to fly from the still wet weapon.

Thessalia called for order again, but the crowd wasn't as easily calmed. Murik smirked at Galessel, and she suppressed a shudder.

"The *Dien-Vek* was never performed upon my daughter!" the queen said with force. "You all would have been informed of this last year, had Murik and his Svellvegan allies not murdered our emissaries." Thessalia pointed at Murik. "He did this to my daughter. He mutilated my daughter during an attack on *The Intrepid* last year. And for that, he will pay."

Queen Kaneti looked to Murik, who shrugged, uncaring.

"While Murik's crimes against the Hidden Lands are great," Queen Kaneti said, "we only have your word on this other...detail. It stands to reason you would be protective of your own daughter. Blaming Murik for the crime is somewhat convenient."

"Is there no one else who will speak for Princess Galessel?" The question came from Spinel Opalforged.

Galessel nodded her thanks to the D'zur battle leader.

As if in response to the question, the floors of the hall began to vibrate with the force of enormous footfalls. At the far end of the hall, walking through the floor-to-ceiling entrance, came the Hidden Land's protector: Soji.

The gryphon surveyed the hall with golden eyes. Many in the crowd cowed from the powerful gaze, others bowed in reverence. "I, Soji of the Ravela nation, sworn protector of the Hidden Lands and champion of the goddess Vanriss, vouches for the innocence and true honor of Galessel, daughter of Thessalia."

The only sound in the hall was a soft chuckling. All assembled turned to find the source, finally settling on Murik.

"Well, I say I did nothing to her, so it's her word against mine. I demand trial by combat, according to Svellvegan law. If she wins, she can kill me. If I win, I'll kill her for being a lying *madlah*, and then I'll submit myself to whatever punishment you wish for me." He turned in a circle, looking at the crowd. "How can you pass up such a generous and fair bargain?"

Galessel was prepared for this eventuality, having discussed various outcomes of this assembly with Clove and Navarre beforehand. Judging by the mortified looks on her parents' faces, they had not.

Her father looked to Navarre, who nodded.

Galessel's mother wasn't so easily calmed. She looked ready to refuse, but Galessel's grandmother, Annalinde, stepped forward and whispered something in her ear. The two whispered back and forth for several minutes before Thessalia nodded and turned to face Galessel.

In a voice that carried across the hall, she asked, "Princess Galessel, do you accept trial by combat according to Svellvegan law? This combat will be to the death unless the loser is granted mercy."

Taking a deep breath to calm her nerves, Galessel looked to her parents, who were still worried, then to Navarre, who was grave but smiled, and finally to Murik, who smirked at her. She knew she didn't have a choice—not if she wanted to stay in the Hidden Lands. Navarre had trained her well this past year. Murik was a troll-trained hack. It wouldn't be easy, but it wouldn't be impossible to win. Besides, she had her gift.

She faced the crowd. "I accept the challenge. I will prove my innocence."

As the fae started to clear a space in the center of the hall, Galessel felt her grandmother's hand on her arm, and she turned to face her. The elder queen looked concerned. It was an emotion she wasn't used to seeing on her grandmother's face.

"Be careful, child. All Svellvega have dark auras, but this one's is red. He uses blood magic. Whatever you do, don't let him draw your blood."

She'd heard rumors, but to have it confirmed made the butterflies in her stomach flutter madly. She counted herself lucky Murik hadn't used that skill on her on *The Intrepid*. He'd had plenty of access to her blood then. The thought of that day still caused her breath to catch in her throat. She forced herself to take a deep breath.

Navarre took her aside, handing her rapier to her. His smile was gone, and worry creased his forehead. "I figured out your trick, *ma chérie*. Your gift is an effective tool, but I'd advise you not to use it."

Galessel felt a bit of her confidence slide. "Why would I not use every advantage to make a quick end to this bastard?" She felt a little hurt.

Navarre took her free hand in his, holding it tightly. "Because I know you can beat him without it. Yes, he's stronger than you, but you're naturally faster and more skilled. Use that against him, and wear him out. If you do use your silver tongue, you'll always question whether or not you could have beaten him without it." He let go of her hand and cupped her chin. "And I know you, Galessel. Cheating is not in your nature."

She felt her eyes fill with tears and tried to blink them away. Navarre was right. At least about not cheating. She prayed he was right about her being able to beat Murik without using her gift.

Jerethon, her personal guard, approached, clearing his throat. "They're ready m'lady." He handed her a fitted leather vest. It was thick but supple. "It was all they would allow you. I'm sorry."

Galessel slipped into the vest and tied it closed. "Thank you, Jerethon."

She took Navarre's hand in her own. "I know your training will see me through, but it wouldn't hurt to pray to Chaun, the god of luck." She smiled. "I won't be long."

Navarre pulled her into a tight embrace and whispered into her hair. "Trust your training, and come back to me." He let her go, but they parted with reluctance.

She stepped back and took another deep breath. "Jerethon, please, show me the way."

Stepping into the area cleared for the fight felt like stepping through a druid's magic fog. Whether it was actually a magic force or her own fear and reluctance hindering her steps, she didn't know, but she didn't like it. She was stronger than this.

Guards rimmed the circle, ready to keep observers out and the fighters in. She was on her own. The guards had been ordered and were honor bound to let the fight play out how it may. Even if that meant her death.

Murik stood across from her, naked to the waist. Cuts and bruises stood out starkly across his torso. A large knot stood out in red and purple relief on his forehead.

One of the guards handed him a rapier. He tested its balance, then proceeded to move through several forms that were showy and meant to intimidate an opponent.

Galessel was sure it would do just that, if the opponent wasn't also trained. To her, it was nothing more than posturing. She felt her confidence rise.

"You can beat this piece of trash, Galey," she said to herself in her best imitation of Clove. "I'm no longer afraid of you, Murik. You can't hurt me." And for the first time, she actually believed it.

Galessel held her rapier in a beginner's ready position and waited. It wouldn't do to show her hand too early.

"I took it easy on you before, little elfling, but now I'm going to kill you in front of your family." Murik smirked as he walked toward her. "What a horrible way to die. I'll make you wish I'd killed you last year," he said quietly so only she could hear. He laughed, sounding deranged. "I'm positively giddy with excitement. Maybe today isn't such a disappointment after all."

Murik lunged at her, but Galessel had been watching his feet and knew which way he was going to move. She dodged him easily but didn't strike back. She wanted to get more of his measure before fully engaging. And she needed to get her heartbeat to calm down. It felt like a dragonling was trying to hatch in her chest.

"What's wrong, elfling? Too scared to try to hit me?" Murik taunted. He moved, feinting before trying to slash at her face.

Galessel leaned back, deflecting his attempt with her sword. Murik pressed the attack, and they traded attacks and parries for a few moments before Galessel broke off, putting some space between them. Murik wasn't quite the hack she'd hoped. He knew some standard moves—ones Galessel had graduated past within months of training with Navarre.

Murik wasn't going to let her rest. He pushed forward, feinting, trying to get her to attack. She parried his sword, batting it aside until she tired of playing. It was likely he too was testing her, but it was time to get this over with.

She stepped in closer, attacking with alternating overhand and underhand attacks. He countered them all. Murik stepped back, swung and spun, trying to catch her off guard, but she'd seen the move coming and stepped in and just to his left, deftly handing off her sword to her off hand, and in the process, lining its tip right up with

Murik's wrist as he came back around. Her sword went right through his wrist. She twisted and pulled it from Murik, spinning away as the Svellvega roared in rage.

"You might have gotten first blood but you won't get the last." He took his sword in his other hand and rushed her, intending, no doubt to bowl her over, but she danced out of his way, slashing him across the back as he passed her.

Navarre had spent many an hour lecturing her on how to overcome an opponent by getting into their head. They were much easier to beat when emotions overrode logic and calm thinking. She'd had no idea it would be so easy to bait Murik.

The second strike had served to calm Murik somewhat, and he approached her with more caution, his sword point held low. Without warning, he lunged again, and Galessel barely dodged the strike meant for her heart.

"Be cautious, Gal. Even an enraged bull still has his instincts." Navarre's admonition echoed in her mind.

"And they're even more dangerous," she whispered to herself.

She moved in, attacking once again, her feet dancing across the hall's stone floors. She spun in, attacked, and spun back out again, always keeping Murik turning in a circle.

Galessel could tell in his eyes when he'd detected the pattern and abruptly switched, spinning in the opposite direction. She brought her sword up and lunged, her sword sliding through Murik's forearm. She pulled up on her sword with all her strength, cutting through tendon and muscle. The sword fell from his now useless hand.

The loss of his sword didn't stop Murik. He lunged at her again, trying to get her in a bear hug. She danced out of his way, slashing him across the chest as she did so.

He tried to grab her sword tip, but she was moving too fast, and it slid through his fist, slicing his already injured hand. Murik was now bleeding freely from multiple wounds. But that only seemed to make him more determined.

He rushed her again, but this time instead of moving out of his way, she moved toward him, ducking and rolling at just the right moment. She came up in the perfect position to slice across the back of his hamstring, cutting the major tendon there. He fell to one knee, his leg unable to properly function.

"Yield," Galessel said from behind him. She kept her sword leveled at his back.

"Never," Murik said, struggling to stand. He hopped on his good leg and turned to face her. "You will have to kill me, *bidjwa*," he spat.

The crowd hissed at the slur.

Galessel had heard him call her that so many times in her nightmares, it no longer had much of an effect on her. She leveled her sword at his throat, and he slapped it away. Again he tried to grab her, but his injured leg couldn't handle his weight and he tipped sideways. As he hopped to regain his balance, Galessel again went low and slashed him across the back of his good knee. Murik went down hard, falling forward onto his hands.

Galessel grabbed a handful of hair, pulling Murik's head back and put her sword across his throat. "Yield." Her hand was steady, but she felt too calm. It would be all too easy to end things here and now. That thought scared her.

Murik smiled at her, his upside-down grin disturbing. "You should hate them as much as I do. I docked your ears on *The Intrepid*, but they banished you just for the way you looked." The crowd gasped at the confession, but Murik didn't seem to care. "You became different and unclean, just like me. And for what? The loss of your ear tips? I'm a dead man—it doesn't matter—but you should continue my work."

Galessel was thrilled with the confession, but Murik's statement about continuing his work didn't make any sense to her. It made her skin crawl. "What do you mean, continue your work? Continue the destruction of the Hidden Lands and the genocide of millions?"

"Yes! Why not? Look at what they did to us. My own father rejected me because of my mixed blood, sold me into slavery, forgetting my very existence. My own people only accepted me out of fear. Even my lover, Davorin, never really respected me—because I was part Anisbarii." He tried to turn his head, but Galessel held it fast.

Murik returned his gaze to her. His eyes were filled with madness. "All I did was damage your beauty, but what they did was far worse." He moved his eyes to look at the crowd. "You! You exiled her, hunted her, and treated her like a criminal, even going so far as to put a bounty on her head! She survived all of that and became better and stronger than before, and it was thanks to me! I made her this way. When I cut her ear tips off, she stopped being a weakling elf, and became worthy of the Svellvega!"

A few in the crowd cheered briefly.

Murik continued, the madness growing. "What the gods created here in the Hidden Lands is flawed. How else do you explain an Anisbarii becoming Svellvega, or the fact that the elves now keep human advisors? This realm is corrupt and must die."

"What was created was created out of love," a soft, but commanding female voice said from what seemed like everywhere at once.

The murmuring of the crowd died. Galessel looked for the source of the voice, but saw nothing. The skin on the back of her neck tightened with unease.

Murik appeared unphased. "Where was that love for me?" he roared. "Where were you when my father killed my mother for bearing me? Where were you when I was cold and alone in the mountains of the trolls? The gods don't love us. We're playthings on a game board to be manipulated for their amusement."

The unseen voice didn't answer.

Queen Kaneti stepped forward, pausing only briefly for the guards to let her through. She stood before Murik and motioned for Galessel to release him. The fight had ended, and Murik was Kaneti's subject. Galessel slowly backed away but didn't let down her guard.

Kaneti knelt on one knee and took Murik's chin in her hand. "You were strong—our people are strong. You were strong enough to have survived your childhood. You could have made your life whatever you wanted, and yet this is what you chose. Every fae is responsible for their own lives. No one forced you to do this—to kill entire races. Therefore, you and you alone will suffer the consequences of your actions." She stood and walked away from Murik, leaving him broken in the circle.

"What has been decreed will be done." The disembodied voice carried physical weight, and more than one fae actually bowed under its pressure. A light flashed at the edge of the cleared circle.

Galessel waited for her eyes to clear from the flash. When they did, a tall woman with dark skin and flowing white hair stood before her and Murik. Long, diaphanous lavender robes cascaded from her shoulders and flowed over her feet onto the floor. The hall was filled with the scent of a forest floor after a spring storm. Thunder rumbled overhead. Flanking her were two large black panthers with feathered wings.

Whispers of "Vanriss," filtered through the crowd.

Galessel immediately dropped to a knee and bowed her head before the goddess of nature.

VANRISS

Chapter 18
Anisbar

The assembled crowd dropped to the floor in worship. Whispers of "All praise to the mother of nature, sacred Vanriss," came from countless lips in a dozen languages.

After the shock of the goddess's appearance faded, Galessel returned her attention to Murik. She didn't trust him not to try something while everyone was distracted by Vanriss.

He did, in fact, try perhaps to flee, but one of Vanriss's panthers mirrored his movement. The cat's eyes began to swirl like whirlpools, and Murik froze in his tracks.

Vanriss seemed not to notice, focusing her attention on the crowd as she spoke. "First things first, I suppose."

Her tone was matter of fact, and she sounded very much like one of Galessel's early tutors, frustrated with her charge's lack of attention. "We did not spend a thousand years creating the fionnagh just so that some *madla mai* with father issues could ruin our creation. You cannot comprehend how long it took me to create the perfect blend of fae and horse. All of that beautiful work—ruined." A crystal tear slid down her face as it darkened from sadness to rage. Lightning flashed and thunder boomed overhead. More than one fae in the crowd cowered.

"I am beyond angry with you, Murik, and I am not the only one." Vanriss started pacing. Her panthers remained where they were, guarding Murik. "Avieth wanted to flood the whole of the Hidden Lands and start over. Reyssa wanted to blind all of the Svellvega, and Ranya wanted to turn you into goldfish, leave you in a desert, and bet on if you'd suffocate or desiccate first. Luckily for all of you, I talked them out of it. And while we cannot immediately bring the centaurs and the nightsteeds back, we will make it right. I have spoken."

Galessel was transfixed by the goddess, the entire crowd was. No one spoke as Vanriss returned to Murik and took his chin in her hand, lifting his face to hers.

Power gathered in the room, swirling like an autumn wind, bringing a bone-deep chill with it. A tornado of red-tinged magic surrounded Murik, and Galessel could almost taste the goddess's rage, it was so strong.

Vanriss spoke, her voice deepening with power. "I, and all of the gods of the Hidden Lands and beyond, do curse you, Murik, son of Kanayda and Filauria. You are now and forever *sikevra*. There is no place in all the realms where you shall find a home. There is no place in all of the realms where you will find peace. There is no place in all the realms where you shall find shelter or compassion. You are banished from the Hidden Lands, and no magic or technology crafted by human, fae, beast, dragon, spirit, angel, or demon will ever allow you entrance. Furthermore, you are no longer fae."

The swirling red magic instantly concentrated around Murik. The Svellvegan began to change. The tips of his ears melted until they were rounded and human in appearance. Murik shuddered as his body changed, becoming somewhat less of what he'd been, and yet, though it must have been painful, he never cried out.

Vanriss stepped away from Murik, and her panthers moved to flank her. The goddess held out her hand, palm outward and said, "You. Are. Exiled."

Murik disappeared. There was no flash. He didn't fade away. He was there one moment. The next: gone.

Galessel let out a breath she hadn't been aware she was holding. It was over. She'd defeated Murik, and now he was gone. But was he still a threat? Where had he gone? Could he still cause trouble in Ashelon?

Her thoughts were interrupted by Vanriss, who stood before Galessel, her hand held out for her. The thunder was gone, replaced with the light music of birdsong. "Let us talk, for there is a ceremony to be performed and then much work to be done."

As the goddess led Galessel back to her parents and friends, Queen Thessalia stepped forward and said, "To all of those assembled, we would be honored if you and yours would stay to witness the *Fallana Sian*."

The crowd, which had not long ago booed her, erupted in cheers. Had Galessel not been holding the hand of a goddess, she was sure she would have fainted. At last, she would be redeemed.

⊗ ⊗ ⊗

Murik's whole body felt like it was on fire. His bones ached and his muscles felt like they would snap as he pushed himself to stand. Curious—his hands were bloody, but the damage that damned elf had done was healed. He could walk, painful as it was, and his left hand worked again. He felt his ears and cursed. They were flattened with rounded edges and his earring was gone.

That bitch of a goddess had really turned him human. He spat on the ground in disgust.

He looked around and found himself unfamiliar with his surroundings. Vanriss had dropped him in the middle of some small town square, in what appeared to be a poor district. Dilapidated buildings surrounded a market square dotted with vegetable stalls and loose fowl. Murik looked closer at some of the signs on the buildings. The writing was fae. But Vanriss had banished him from the Hidden Lands. That meant she'd dropped him somewhere in Ashelon.

He smiled. Was Vanriss really that stupid?

Murik started walking toward a small coach for hire. He might not be able to get back into the Hidden Lands, but that didn't mean he couldn't send another group of Hammer Guardians in to finish the job.

A rock hit him in the back of the head, hard. His hand came away bloody when he felt the knot already forming. Another rock followed, and another. One hit him hard enough to drop him to his knees. When the stars finally cleared, he found himself surrounded by an angry mob of fae.

A young gnome with a beard that barely reached his chest stepped forward, brandishing a cobbler's hammer in his hand. "We heard what you did, *sikevra*. Vanriss may have spared your life, but that doesn't mean we have to. You killed our blacksmith and his mate. They were expecting a foal this spring!"

Murik tried to shield his head as the cobbler drew back his arm, but someone strong grabbed his arms, pinning them to his side. The glint of the sun off the hammer was the last thing he saw.

Chapter 19
Anisbar

Galessel smoothed the royal blue silk gown over her hips. Simply cut, it flowed around her form to pool at her bare feet. Because the *Fallana Sian* was meant to reconnect one to the land and people one was banished from, nothing must separate that person from the earth. In fact, no one at the ceremony would wear shoes of any kind.

She pulled a silver belt from her dresser and fastened it low on her hips. A simple silver diadem sat across her brow, and her hair flowed long and free down her back.

Galessel heard the ringing of Clove's hooves before her friend knocked on the door and let herself in.

"Are you ready, m'lady?"

Galessel turned to her friend, shaking her head. "When did you become so formal, Clove?" Her friend was even dressed a bit more conservatively than normal, in purple pants gathered at the knee, and a green blouse cinched with a yellow leather belt styled with leaves.

Clove smiled mischievously. "I thought I better try to be serious before the ceremony starts. Otherwise there's no chance!"

Galessel laughed, happy to see Clove hearty and hale. She bowed to her friend. "Then by all means, let's." She straightened and held out her hand. "Come, Lady Clove, let us away to the ceremony ere we be late."

Neither could hold back the giggles as they left Galessel's room.

Galessel stood alone in the shadow of the ancient, towering oak trees surrounding a large meadow in the middle of sacred Anisbarii lands. A large, circular stone platform appeared to emerge organically from the meadow's floor at the far end of the glade. Legend said it was sung into place by Druids in a time lost even to elven memory.

Normally a place of quiet picnics and joyous ceremonies, this day it would witness a more somber one.

The glade had filled with emissaries and royalty who had initially gathered to see a different sort of justice done. Satyrs stood next to D'zur, raising the scent of thyme and lavender from the herbs crushed beneath their hooves and feet. Pixies and brownies made faces at each other, while fairies fluttered above the heads of wood nymphs and selkies. Members of the Seelie and Unseelie courts stood in truce, though far apart from one another. Redcaps kept hold of their zephyr steeds on the edge of the meadow, their caps dry. Soji sat tall and regal behind the stone, a towering presence and the gods' witness to what was to come. Among all of them mingled the elves of the Anisbarii, tall and proud, talking among their guests and subtly arranging everyone into a spiral leading to the platform.

As the last guest was positioned, Clove, the pistons in her prosthetic ankles hissing softly, slipped in to take her place on the stone next to Navarre, Eirsal, and Samga.

Galessel watched as Navarre looked to the trees for her. Her cheeks warmed when their eyes met and he winked at her. She smiled and blew a kiss in return.

Galessel's family emerged from the trees, her two sisters first: Miniel, dark of hair and tan of skin like their father, holding the hand of her daughter, Talindra, and Gilrin, blonde and fair like their mother. The king and queen of Anisbar followed their daughters and granddaughter onto the stone.

The crowd fell completely silent. Galessel's parents were the epitome of regal, dressed in matching royal blue and silver garb, their vine-like silver crowns glinting on their brows. They took their place on the stone platform.

Once again, Queen Thessalia addressed the crowd. "Beings of the Hidden Lands, thank you for staying to witness this most important ceremony. As you now know, our daughter, Princess Galessel, was brutally attacked and permanently scarred by the Svellvega pirate, Murik. He wanted to destroy the Hidden Lands, to tear us apart, but he has done quite the opposite. He's given us a reason to come together and celebrate our strength."

The crowd erupted in cheers and whistles but quieted again at the raised hand of the queen. "In ages past, the *Fallana Sian* was held to welcome back one who was wrongly banished from our lands, to restore them to the land, to their home and to their people. Today, we hold the *Fallana Sian* to show our support for one who was wronged, to show her, and those who would tear us down, that what they did, we do not condone, nor will we allow their actions to go unanswered."

The assembled guests again raised up a cheer, their bare feet stamping the ground. Again, the queen held up a hand to quiet them, a wry smile on her face.

King Valandil stepped forward and called to his daughter. "Princess Galessel, come take your place with your family."

Galessel glided out of the shadows of the trees and approached the stone with her head held high. The rows of fae parted to let her through, and soft whispers of love and support followed in her wake. None mentioned the state of her ears, though the feelings of horror at what had been done to her, awakened by her earlier duel with Murik, could be felt throughout the sacred space.

Her father took her hands and kissed her cheek as she stepped up on the stone. He then guided her to her place in the center of the stone.

"Assembled guests," King Valandil began, "kings and queens of the Fae. Princess Galessel is the wrongful victim of the *Dien-Vek*. Though her ear tips were taken, her spirit was not. She stands before you as the beloved daughter of the Anisbarii kingdom and hero to the

Hidden Lands. We hereby declare that her status is not diminished by what has been done to her."

He turned to smile at Galessel before continuing. "Revered Mother, will you please step forward?"

From the depths of the forest, Galessel's grandmother appeared, her silver hair gathered in a long braid that flowed down her back. She was crowned with a simple rose-silver diadem. Before her, she carried something delicate on a blue silk pillow. The crowd bowed to her as one. The former elven queen stood quietly until the crowd rose.

"My friends, today we ask for you to aid us with your magic and your blessing," Queen Mother Annalinde said. "We would restore what has been taken from our kin with these silver ear tips."

Quiet "ahs" could be heard through the crowd as Galessel's grandmother held up the pillow and what it carried for all to see. Finely wrought silver wire ear tips gleamed brightly against the blue of the pillow. Small gems caught the light in their wire cages, while tight spirals formed an intricate design within the pointed tips.

The aged elf walked to stand at the end of the spiral. Bowing her head, she said a silent blessing over the tips before passing the pillow to the D'zur battle leader.

Spinel Opalforged placed her rough hand over the tips and mouthed a quiet prayer before passing it on to the Druid next to her. From one creature to the next, the pillow passed along the spiral, each race bestowing its own form of blessing or prayer on the delicate ears.

As the magic rose in the glade, the air started to shimmer, and Galessel found it difficult to hold back tears. The pillow was eventually passed up to Clove on the stone platform, and Galessel's childhood friend placed her hand on the tips, smiling at Galessel as she whispered a blessing. Galessel's sisters did the same, but unlike Galessel, they did not hold back gentle tears.

Finally, the pillow made its way to the king and queen, who each took a delicate tip and moved to stand on either side of their daughter.

Queen Thessalia's voice rang through the quiet meadow. "Beings of the Hidden Lands, with these ear tips, we restore our daughter's honor and her dignity. Let none in this realm, or any other, ever doubt her standing as a princess of the Anisbarii."

A wild cheer rose up from formerly somber meadow as the king and queen each placed an ear tip over Galessel's rounded ears.

As the silver touched her skin, all the blessings and love given by the assembled fae spread like warm water over Galessel and tears fell, unchecked, down her cheeks. Her mother and father hugged her, whispering their own blessings to her before letting her go.

Soji, quiet until now, raised their giant wings and proclaimed, "As guardian of the Hidden Lands, and representative of the gods, we declare Galessel, third of the daughters of Thessalia, though maimed, was never *sikevra*. She is once again whole and will speak for us in the courts of the Hidden Lands."

Galessel was stunned. She wasn't sure she heard Soji correctly, but she didn't have time to process what the gryphon had said.

Soji bent down and nudged her in the back with their beak.

"Turn around, Galessel. I have a gift for you."

Galessel turned and faced the immense gryphon.

"You came to our defense and stood resolute in the face of certain death when tested by our magic. You are truly worthy of being our emissary." Two tears fell from Soji's eyes. One landed on each ear.

Galessel's ears tingled, a mix of tiny pinpricks and cool flashes danced along the edges.

When the tingling subsided, Soji said, "Now you are truly whole."

Galessel raised her hands to her ears, feeling where the rounded edges once were, and instead finding a seamless join between flesh and silver. She looked at Soji, and lost for words, hugged the gryphon as she sobbed with joy.

It took her a moment to remember she was surrounded by the rulers of the Hidden Lands, but when she did, she wiped the tears from her cheeks, moved back from the gryphon, and bowed low.

"Honored protector, I do not have the words to express my gratitude to you for this gift. I am deeply honored, and I vow to serve you to the best of my abilities, always."

Galessel turned around to face the assembled fae. Her life had turned around drastically in the last day, and she still wasn't sure it was real. But if it was, she would embrace it.

She stepped forward, bowing to the assembled crowd, who cheered once again.

She let the crowd cheer for a moment, letting their energy wash over her. It had been too long since she felt whole, and fully like herself. Holding up her hand,

Galessel motioned for the crowd to quiet. They did, slowly.

"Honored friends and guests, I am humbled by your presence here, and by your willingness to join together in a time of tribulation. The Hidden Lands and her people have lost much at the hands of Queen Victoria of Ashelon."

The crowd booed, many crying out for war against the humans—to wipe them out.

Galessel asked for quiet again but had to yell to be heard. "I understand your pain, and your need for vengeance, but I ask you, is answering one genocide with another, a weight you're ready to carry?"

The crowd quieted.

"Queen Victoria must answer for the wrongs she's committed against our people. Not only for the genocide of the centaurs and nightsteeds, but for the maltreatment of our kin in Ashelon. We must stand up for those who still struggle. It is not the humans as a whole who we must fight, but those who hold dominion over the masses. The royal court of Ashelon is to blame, yes, but also the lords of industry who enslave elementals and our fae kin to run their factories. Greed is the enemy.

"Victoria seeks to rule not only the mortal realm, but ours as well, and though she lost this time, she will not stop. I ask for a continuation of this truce between all assembled. Together, we can keep the Hidden Lands whole, and bring Victoria to justice!"

In the silence that followed, Galessel watched as the gathered rulers sized each other up, weighing her words. She'd taken a calculated risk in assuming the truce would hold. There was no discernible signal, but the tension which had been building suddenly broke, and the clearing was filled with cheers.

Galessel sighed with relief, stepping back from the edge of the platform.

Fairies and pixies took to the air, spreading pixie dust over everyone. The D'zur began to sneeze, being somewhat allergic to pixie dust, but did not grumble. Instead, they began to clamour for ale to wash away the dust.

Navarre stepped forward, bowing to the king and queen before taking Galessel's hand. "I would be honored if you would allow me to stay by your side as guard and confidant in your new role."

"I would love nothing more," Galessel replied. She pulled Navarre to her and kissed him, to the delight and surprise of the crowd.

"Hey, you two, I think you've shocked your parents enough," Clove said, pushing the two of them apart before hugging Galessel herself. "Congratulations—on everything, Galey. Today was a long time coming."

"Thank you my friend, and thank you for standing by my side through everything."

Clove brushed off the compliment, but her ears stood tall, a sign she was happy.

Eirsal was next, bowing formally before Galessel raised him with a laugh. "Princess, I too will stand by your side." He glanced uneasily at the redcaps at the edge of the meadow. "But may I respectfully ask to never have to go into Unseelie lands again?" he whispered.

"Of course, Eirsal. I hope that none of us will be asked to visit there any time soon," she whispered back. What Eirsal and his group had endured still made Galessel cringe. Outside of losing Morgan, his group had faced the worst of all of them.

Samga approached and gave Galessel a hug. The archer smiled, but it didn't penetrate the sadness in her eyes. "Morgan would be proud of you, as am I," she said.

Galessel hugged her tight. "Morgan's sacrifice will never be forgotten, Samga. You have my word."

Samga nodded before quickly fading into the approaching crowd of well-wishers.

The sacred glade was once again turned into a place of joyous frivolity as plates of food and flagons of wine and mead were brought in and passed around to the guests. A group of satyrs gathered to play the pipes and drums, two Seelie princes added their voices to the music, and soon the crowd danced along.

Overwhelmed by the day's events, Galessel bided her time, graciously making small talk with those who came to wish her well or give their thoughts on how to deal with Ashelon, all the while waiting for a chance to quietly slip away. As if reading her thoughts, her grandmother appeared, rescuing her from the renowned gnome professor who had lapsed into a treatise on the application of powdered hydronium as a lubricant in gear-works.

"Excuse me, Professor Fizzlespring, but may I steal my granddaughter for a moment?" the elder elf interjected in a rare pause in the gnome's speech.

The professor hurriedly straightened his multi-lensed spectacles and bowed to the former elf queen. "Of—of course, your highness, of course!" he stammered. "Princess, I trust you will bring up the matter of the shortage of powdered hydronium should you happen to talk to the D'zur of Freedonia during your new assignment?"

Galessel nodded. "Of course, Professor. I will make it a priority. Now if you will excuse me?"

"By all means, Princess. Bright blessings to you," Fizzlespring said as he bowed.

She and her grandmother made a hasty exit to the shadow of the trees before anyone else could corner Galessel.

"Thank you, Grandmother, for rescuing me. While I understand the basic principles of hydronium and how it's used in the outside world, Fizzlespring has a knack for turning even a basic explanation into a four-day lecture."

Annalinde laughed. "I thank the Goddess he was just a babe when I sat on the throne. I know it's only out of respect for the gnome clans that your mother doesn't ban him from the kingdom just for talking too much!"

She sobered somewhat and took Galessel's hands in hers. "Dear one, I know what was done to you was horrible, and I'm so proud of you for staying strong. Remember today, and the love and support shown to you by all those of the Hidden Lands. You are young yet, and your trials are not over, but I know you will prevail."

Galessel nodded and traced her new ear tips with her fingers. "I have you to thank for these, don't I?" Her grandmother smiled, her eyes crinkling at the corners. "They're beautiful. Thank you."

Her grandmother gathered her into a hug, stroking Galessel's ebony hair. "Soji's magic was great, and the blending of your ears with my silver tips is flawless. And yet, I wish I could restore your ears to their true form, or even grant you the blessing of a permanent glamour. I curse the comet for destroying that part of our magic."

Her grandmother stepped back and spit on the ground. "Asher was always a troublemaking god, and now that he controls half the world through the Queen of Ashelon, he's even worse. Watch yourself, dear one. I fear there may be more trouble yet."

Galessel sighed. "I fear you may be right, though I have some ideas that may help to bridge the gap between the Hidden Lands and Ashelon. And bring justice to Victoria."

"As I knew you would." Her grandmother smiled and took her hand. "Now come, enough of politics and intrigue. I have some of last year's prize Ebony Rose beans stashed away. Let me make you a cup of coffee before you sneak away to bed."

Galessel let herself be led away gratefully. A cup of coffee, especially one brewed from the Ebony Rose variety would be a fitting end to a very eventful day.

Chapter 20
Anisbar

Galessel took a deep breath, inhaling the palace garden's fresh floral scents as she walked along the path to meet her friends. The coffee trees were just coming into bloom, and their stimulating scent wafted down over the palace grounds.

The last few weeks had been a series of grueling negotiations among some of the Hidden Lands' most stubborn races. Queen Kaneti was the worst of them, but in some ways, Galessel couldn't blame her. She was trying to lead her people into a new era after the untimely death of her husband, ending her people's isolation in DawnGuard. Changing the perception of her people as ruthless, violent raiders, a reputation built up over millennia, would not be easy.

In the end, Galessel was confident the Svellvega would be welcomed—if Kaneti was true to her word and stopped her people from raiding. They could prove to be valuable in the times to come.

A trading pact with the D'zur, for a material the Svellvega call glass-steel, would go far in helping change the Svellvega's reputation. Glass-steel was a material new to all but the elves of DawnGuard. A form of ice that did not melt and was harder than steel would have many applications, and the D'zur were interested in seeing what they could do with it. The Svellvega seemed to have it in abundance.

Galessel stroked a new ear tip and shrugged off thoughts of the Svellvega. The silver tip of her ear was warm to the touch, and she could actually feel sensation with it. Whether it was her grandmother's crafting or Soji's magic that made it so, she didn't know, but she was still getting used to it.

She heard her friends chatting in the gazebo ahead and picked up her pace to join them. After dealing with difficult fae for days without a break, she was looking forward to relaxing with everyone. Especially Navarre.

"Galey!" Clove's ears perked up as Galessel came into view. She motioned to an empty chair between herself and Navarre at the round table. Eirsal, Samga, and N'hena sat opposite them. "Come sit down. Coffee just arrived."

The smell of her grandmother's freshly brewed coffee was even more of a pick-me-up than the scent of the coffee blossoms. She sat down gratefully and cradled a warm cup between her hands.

"Navarre was just telling us your father asked him to be captain of the guard," Clove stated as if she were tattling.

Navarre looked slightly guilty at this news. "I have not given him my answer yet. I told him of my promise to you, and that we would need to talk first."

Galessel thought about it for a moment. Navarre's promise and her father's offer weren't necessarily mutually exclusive. "What if you could do both?" she asked. "As Soji's emissary, I've been returned, essentially, to my duties as an ambassador for the Hidden Lands. And, as a princess of Anisbar, I will require the services of the Royal Guard. My station should allow me to pick my guards, so I pick you."

She sat back, smug, and smiling.

Navarre returned her smile, saying, "As you wish, *ma chérie.*"

"So that's settled," Clove said, clearly satisfied.

Galessel looked across at Samga, who appeared more centered than she'd seen her since Morgan's death. "Samga, your skills as an archer would be welcome in the Guard, should you wish to stay."

Samga folded her hands into her sleeves. "I am honored that you think my skills so worthy, Galessel, but with your permission, I think I will return to Vallanon. There is a peace there with the oak-kin that I believe will help me clear my head and lighten my heart."

"Of course, Samga," Galessel replied. "We will miss you. Please know you are welcome here, always. I hope you find the peace you seek."

Navarre put his hand on Samga's shoulder. "I grieve with you, my friend. Morgan will always be with us. When you are ready to return, we will be here."

Samga nodded but said nothing.

"Eirsal, what about you? You, too, are welcome within the ranks of the Guard or another position of your choosing," Galessel said.

Eirsal grinned, the roots of his wings turning purple with mischief. "I thought I might visit SoulScar again."

Everyone looked at him for a moment before he burst out laughing at his joke. King Damháin had sworn to kill the sylph should he ever set foot in SoulScar again. "Actually," he said when his mirth had faded, "I have no idea what I want to do, but I don't think I want to settle down anywhere."

"You know—" N'hena started. "I have a need for a few new crew members on *The Intrepid*." She winked at Eirsal, her wings flushing pink.

Eirsal blushed. "Well, I guess crewing an airship isn't technically settling down. I suppose I could give it a try."

N'hena playfully punched him in the arm. "You'll have to do more than try if you're to make it on my ship, mister." She laughed.

Before he could retort, Clove said, "Those all sound like perfectly nice options. I mean they're all very nice. And tame. And, well, safe." Clove's ears were cocked in a way that said she was up to no good.

"Oh no. I know that look, Clove. You're about to get me in trouble again, aren't you?" Galessel asked. She both loved and hated that about her friend.

Samga startled them all by saying, "No, Galessel, she's about to get *all* of us into trouble again."

Samga was not wrong. Clove was happiest when she could rope multiple people into her schemes.

"I kind of like trouble," Eirsal said.

N'hena nodded, adding, "Aye, a little trouble is good for the soul. And the coin purse."

Navarre looked skeptical. "What did you have in mind, Clove?"

Clove's ears perked up, and she grinned. "We all work really well together, and it would be a shame for all of this talent to go to waste. Things around here seem pretty well in hand, especially after Galey's work these past weeks. But Ashelon is still a mess."

Galessel added, "There has been talk of recruiting humans to populate the lands poisoned by cold-iron. Even though Soji has managed to reduce it to rust, the fae won't be able to live there for hundreds of years. There are many less fortunate in Ashelon who would welcome the opportunity to be out from under Victoria's thumb. I'm sure I can convince my parents to let me lead that effort. And," she paused, "someone needs to keep an eye on Victoria. You know she's not going to take this defeat lying down."

There were nods of agreement around the table.

"Then it's decided. Let's meet back here in a month's time, and then it's back to Ashelon we go!" Clove held up her mug.

Everyone but Samga followed suit. They paused, unsure if the archer would join them. With a sigh and a sad smile, she held up her mug. "Morgan would be cross if she knew I wasn't going to join in. You are going to need someone to watch your backs," she said.

They clinked their mugs together. Navarre said, "*Sláinte!*" It was Morgan's favorite toast. They all echoed him, becoming more somber with her memory. "You know another thing Morgan would be cross with us about? If we didn't all go get very drunk tonight," Navarre mused.

"Then what are we waiting for?" Clove bounded from her seat. "I know a great little pub not far from here." The faun sauntered off down the garden path.

The others followed Clove, but Galessel hung back with Navarre, wanting a moment alone with him.

She took his hand and looked deep into his brown eyes. "I know I've said this many times over the past few weeks, but thank you. Thank you for helping me in Arturia, for training me, and being by my side through all of this. I couldn't have survived without you."

"You would have survived, *ma chérie*. You are the strongest person, eh, elf I know. You can do anything you set your mind to. My sword is yours to command, as is my heart."

He kissed her, and the whole world seemed to disappear but for the two of them.

Epilogue

Queen Victoria sat near the window in her private chambers, embroidering a piece of linen, her breathing apparatus long forgotten in a far corner. Her illness had subsided with Lord Davorin's absence. She did not think it was a coincidence.

Asher himself had appeared a fortnight ago to tell her of the failure of the Hammer Guardians, shattering her dreams of dominating the realm of the fae. But the god of chaos had brought a bit of welcome news, as well. The Svellvegan pirate, Murik, had survived the debacle and was currently on a steamer ship headed to the cold climes of Rusvarag in the north.

If she could intercept him, he might prove to be a valuable asset, even more so now that he was human.

Murik would have critical intelligence and insight into the Hidden Lands.

But she needed to be cautious. Anyone willing to destroy their own world out of spite would need careful handling.

There was a knock at her chamber door. "Yes," she responded.

Her chamberlain entered, a smile on his wrinkled face. "A messenger has come, your highness. He says our operative has made contact with Murik, and the pirate has agreed to your terms, but he wants a ship."

Victoria smiled, laying aside her embroidery of Asher's symbol—four crossed, double headed arrows with a teardrop in the middle.

"Send word that Murik can have his ship, as long as he brings me Princess Galessel's head."

The chamberlain nodded and backed out of the door, closing it.

When one door closes, the gods open another. She would get what she wanted, one way or another.

THE END

GLOSSARY

Dien-Vek An elven banishment ritual involving the removal of the tips of an elf's ears.

Fallana Sian An elven forgiveness ceremony often held to reverse the banishment from *Dien-Vek*.

Fionnagh A magical pillar created by the gods which is the source of magic and the magical beings within the Hidden Lands.

Madla-mai A strong elven curse, similar in meaning to 'son-of-a-bitch'.

Nodgoddim The common tongue of the Hidden Lands

Ravela A bird-like humanoid creature with brightly colored feathers. Flocks of ravela often play off the bows of fae airships.

R'vikki An intelligent cat-like race.

Sikevra An outcast. An elf subjected to the *Dien-Vek* becomes *sikevra*.

About the Author

Carolyn Kay is a scientist by day, and an author, dancer, knitter, and herbalist by night. She's attempting to raise two fine felines with the help of her husband, Chaz Kemp. (The results are mixed. *Looking at you, Sif*) She also occasionally channels a fae changeling, named Cinder. You can catch up on her latest shenanigans at carolynkayauthor.com, or on Twitter @bewitchinghips.

About the Artist

Chaz Kemp is the self-described Art Monkey Supreme behind all of the fabulous art of Ashelon. His origins are clouded in fantastical mystery. Was he found under a rock as his mother claims, or is he really a fae son of the King of the Faeries? We may never know. What we do know is that Chaz is an accomplished artist, musician, actor, and fur-kid father. You can find him at ChazKemp.com and support his work at Patreon.com\chazkemp.

www.ingramcontent.com/pod-product-compliance
Lightning Source LLC
Chambersburg PA
CBHW031942110726
47902CB00001B/264